# IN THE LAND OF THE SALMON

## - A Novel of Alaska -

By

Joshua Keil

**LONE WOLF**
B O O K S

ISBN 978-1-57833-758-3

Cover art: Peter Strain, www.peterstrain.co.uk
Book Design: Carmen Maldonado, Todd Communications
The typeface for this book was set in Times New Roman

First printing August 2020

Printed in China
through **Alaska Print Brokers**, Anchorage, Alaska.

Published by:

**LONE WOLF**
BOOKS

www.joshuakeil.com

Distributed by:
Todd Communications
611 E. 12th Ave.
Anchorage, Alaska 99501-4603
Phone: (907) 274-TODD (8633) • Fax: (907) 929-5550
WWW.ALASKABOOKSANDCALENDARS.COM • sales@toddcom.com
with other offices in Juneau and Fairbanks, Alaska

# Table of Contents

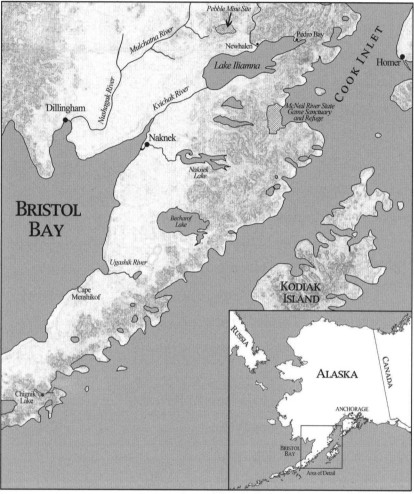

Bristol Bay and Environs

# Prologue

I do not want to close my eyes again.

When I do, I see nothing but water.

When I awoke this morning in a strange bed, I reached for my watch but couldn't read it. I have relied on reading glasses almost constantly since reaching my forties, and that happened more than a quarter of a century ago. Holding the cheap Timex at arm's length, I saw that it was almost four in the morning.

Briefly, I thought about getting out of bed. It was not too early to start an Alaskan summer day—the days are now long—but I decided against it. The cabin was cold, and I reminded myself that I had been dreaming because I had been trying to remember. So, rather than putting the image behind me, I closed my eyes and immersed myself in the storm.

A monstrous wave thrust the bow of the boat high in the air. I could almost feel my stomach lurch as the small craft crested the wave and fell toward the trough on the other side. And then it happened. The boom. The jarring, pounding boom of the hull striking the sand. The young Jim LaBerg that I remember—the boy I once was, so confident, so strong—gunned the throttle with no response. I strained against the ship's wheel, but it was hard over. As the sea lifted the boat again, I sensed the hopelessness of the situation. The boat fell. Another boom. Cracking noises emanated from the fiberglass hull. I resigned myself to the fact that the boat was doomed, but I refused to let Shenandoah die.

"We have to abandon ship!" the young version of myself yelled to the woman, reaching for her with an outstretched hand. Seawater swamped the stern and came in through the cabin door. She came to me with terror in her eyes. "We'll swim ashore!" I yelled over the tumult of the pounding wind, knowing full well that a body cannot live long in the frigid waters of Bristol Bay.

We waded through knee-high water grabbing anything to steady ourselves against the violent lurching of the boat. On deck, I didn't know what to do. Could we jump into the wall of water? I looked at Shenan. She looked at me. I looked past her at a sunlit valley of water between two waves. It was almost beautiful.

"Please, God," I prayed.

"What are you doing, Jim?"

"I'm praying," I yelled over the sound of the wind. My faith rose to unparalleled levels. I grew angry at the storm, and at the evil forces that sent it. A wave hit us with the force of a small car and thrust us against the cabin. Regaining my feet on the tossing, turning, slippery deck, I yelled, "We are not going to die today!" Then I remembered the words of Jesus when he spoke to the storm. I shouted at the storm from the spinning, floundering vessel, "Peace, be still!"

"Peace, be still," I mumbled aloud, laying there in bed, and the sound of my own voice returned me to the present.

Regaining a sense of my whereabouts—of the cold, small cabin and the lumpy, short bed—I tried to observe my dream dispassionately. It is difficult to tease apart the memory from the dream, but it always stops at the same place. I always wake up when I say the words. Always before the end.

I looked at my watch again. Four Thirty now. I rose and sat on the edge of the bed. My back hurt more than usual. Perhaps it was the mattress. It was my first night in a one-room cabin overlooking Lake Iliamna, and I wonder how many nights I will sleep here. Certainly at least a week. A task awaits me, and the task has been delayed.

I have come to this tiny village of Pedro Bay, a town on the shores of Alaska's biggest lake, a town not too far from my own home on the western side of the lake, to talk about the mine. The Pebble Mine. A thing I have heard about and read about ad nauseum. A gold and copper mine that some developer or another has been trying to build for more than a decade. A mine that contains minerals worth at least tens of billions of dollars. Maybe more. A mine that sits at the headwaters of the region's rivers—rivers that run to the ocean at Bristol Bay, the scene of the largest sockeye salmon run in the world. The intense, friend-on-friend, family-splitting debate centers on the wastewater the mine would generate. The developers say they would build dams to prevent the toxic water from leaking into the watershed—dams that would have to last forever. I have talked about and written about these dams many times, but I recently took a trip that changed my thinking on the subject. I saw something that dropped a burning coal of fear in my gut.

As I dressed, feeling the chill in my knees, I rehearsed in my mind what I would say at the rally. My words felt hollow and mundane. They lacked meaning. They were too... me... too scientific.

I put the speech behind me. After all, I had been told that the rally had been delayed a week. And it's hard to think when the muscles between your ribs are shivering. I knew that I would not feel warm until I put my boots on and started a fire. I felt groggy and eyed the coffee pot on the wood stove. I needed caffeine to dissipate the cobwebs in my mind and to dispel the nagging dream.

My enlarged knuckles ached when I fumbled with the matches. Opening the hatch on the stove, I reached in with a burning match. When I blew on the kindling, a wall of flames flashed into life and the monstrous wave rose before my eyes again. "Peace, be still," I muttered.

*Am I really going to do this?* I blew harder until the larger log burst into flames. *Why should I tell the story now when I have not done so all these years?* My thoughts returned the answer. *Because you're running out of time.*

After pouring coffee grounds into the pot and setting it on the stove, I turned and eyed the laptop computer sitting on the small desk near the window overlooking the lake. This would not be my first book. For more than thirty years, I have been a spokesman for the wilderness in books, newspapers, interviews, and government hearings. But I have never written anything so personal. Occasionally, I have been asked if I ever considered settling down with a family. My usual answer is that my life in the wilderness is not conducive to one. I don't bother to tell them that I have been infertile since a young age. And for some curious reason, I don't tell them that there had been a woman in my life. But I will tell them now. I can't tell what Bristol Bay means to me without telling her story.

When my good friend, Finn Nickolai, met me at the plane dock today he asked why I had never written of my time as a fisherman on Bristol Bay. I didn't have a good answer. I know Finn well. He is a member of the Pedro Bay Corporation, one of the many Alaska Native Village Corporations. He and his colleagues control a large portion of the land around the proposed mining site. They have been the mine's biggest roadblock. Literally. They denied a request to build a road across their land. That didn't stop the mining company, though. They've now planned a more circuitous route over the lake.

Given his Russian last name, I'm often tempted to ask Finn if he is a descendent of Old Man Pedtrushko, for whom Pedro Bay is named, but I know the Russian period is a delicate subject.

"We need that story now more than ever," the middle-aged Dena'ina man told me. "You know what the Pebble Mine will do to the salmon."

"You mean what it *could* do," I said, more gruffly than I intended. I feel that everything I say sounds like that now.

"We are trying to tell the story of Bristol Bay, of the salmon, and the lives they support."

"And?"

"And you told me once of your time as a fisherman. I felt your connection to the sea."

"I hate the sea. There are reasons why I stopped being a fisherman."

"But you can bring attention to the salmon. Many people enjoy your writings about the wild places."

"What exactly are you suggesting?"

"That you tell the people what Bristol Bay means to you. It will help in our fight against the mine. It will bring awareness."

"Bristol Bay is a hundred and fifty miles from here."

"But all the people—the people on the bay and the people here on the lake—would be affected by the mine."

I wondered what the story of one fisherman could do that all the other stories could not. Besides, no one seemed to care about the words of an old white man anymore. I told Finn as much.

"People love your stories. And people trust you. That is why the things you said about the mine not hurting the fish meant so much. If you truly feel the way you do now, your voice is very important."

"I'm not going to tell the story in a speech."

"But you can write about it."

"Nonsense."

"You have time. You have all week."

I suspected then that he purposefully withheld news of the delay until I landed. "Did you corner me into this?"

He shrugged.

"Well, I'm not going to fly home now, and spend all the money and carbon that would entail."

"Then you have nothing to do."

"I'm the region's Wildlife Trooper. I have plenty to do."

"Such as?"

"Check permits. Inspect the landfill."

"And write about Bristol Bay," he added.

"Why are you badgering me?"

"If you don't do it for me," Finn said, "do it for her."
I realized, then, that I must have told Finn more about my time as a fisherman than I remembered.

"I'll think about it."

"Good. We need your words in the fight."

As I sat here warming my hands in the small cabin behind Finn's house, I cursed my friend for making me do this. But as my body warmed and my thoughts churned over the material, I had to admit that it was something I had put off for far too long. For many reasons. Now that I have a fire and coffee and plenty of time, I'm plunging into the depths of Bristol Bay for the thousandth time in my life.

# Chapter 1

# The Sea-Nymph

It was 1969, my second season as a commercial fisherman, when I was twenty-two years old. Standing on the bow of Nushagak Joe's fishing boat, I felt the coarseness of the line of rope in my hands. We slid over the choppy water toward a friend's boat, which lay at anchor in a small cove outside Dillingham. Our intention was to tie the two boats together to share dinner with familiar people, but the person I spied sitting on the bow of the other boat was a stranger.

She was a young woman, reading on the bow of the *Nereid*, her back against the berthing compartment, her long legs dangling over the edge. Black hair blew straight behind her in the stiff sea breeze. She wore tan corduroy pants, a baggy blue sweatshirt, and a necklace made of thick brown beads. Her feet were bare. As she swung her legs back and forth, her toes skimmed the water like dragonflies hunting for food.

"Hello, there!" Joe cried out. The old Yup'ik man in the cabin behind me owned the boat and was my only companion on the *Mikilak*. The young woman turned toward us, her wind-blown hair partially obscuring her face. I stood motionless, line in hand, sliding closer, her face growing clearer. I was struck by her light hazel eyes, her delicate nose and tall forehead. I had never seen such a beautiful woman before, neither in Alaska nor in Washington, and I had been no place else.

I don't know what I was doing—staring like a fool I suppose—and maybe that is why her face erupted into a broad smile. I gestured with the line as if to say, "I'm about to throw this to you." She put her book down and stood abruptly, steadying herself for the catch.

As we waited for the boats to close, my thoughts turned to how I might appear to her. I was glad I decided not to wear a shirt under my bib overalls that day. I had spent the entire winter studying at Washington State College but had simultaneously worked for the Park Service building a remote latrine. The work of carrying a thousand cement blocks up the steep mountain honed my arms and shoulders, and I hoped that it showed. My brown hair had grown long and curly on top. I wished now that I had paid for a haircut in town, but I hadn't expected to see a woman during six weeks of fishing on the far edge of the world.

I tossed the line to her. She caught it, ran it once around the cleat, and awkwardly threw it back to me. Catching it, I took a strain on the line and closed our vessels with every pull, striving, of course, to make my muscles work as hard as possible. She stood motionless and watched, working hard to keep the hair out of her face. The black strands darted and shifted in the capricious wind like wild animals trying to escape. They nearly covered her face except for the crevice held open in front of her eyes. And those golden eyes just stared at me, like eyes peeking through a veil.

I pulled harder until our boats slammed into one another, and the crash nearly threw us overboard.

"Easy up there!" the *Nereid's* captain yelled from somewhere behind the pilot house.

"Sorry, Phillip," I yelled, quickly spinning the line around the bow cleat. My skipper, the old Native man whom everyone called Nushagak Joe, cut our engine and stepped out of the pilot house to talk with Phillip. They were old friends.

Only a few feet separated me from the young woman. She spoke first. "Can you do me a favor?"

"Sure."

"Can you show me how to tie the knot?"

"I should probably get to know you first."

She rolled her eyes. "In your dreams. No, I mean the knot on that thing—what do you call it?"

"The cleat."

"Yeah, that. But don't let them see us doing it." She glanced in the direction of the two skippers. They stood on the opposite end of the boat, which was—according to regulations—only thirty-two feet away. Already in conversation, they paid no attention to us. "I'm trying to prove to my uncle that I can do all the man's work on a boat. He asked if I could tie a cleat this morning and I said that I could. I've been practicing all day and it turns out that it's not as easy as it looks."

"So, you lied to him?"

She scrunched her face. "Yeah, I guess so."

I laughed, then got down on one knee. She crouched beside me with her back toward the two older men. "It can be confusing," I said. "The trick is knowing how to twist

the line at the same time you're making a figure-eight."
I untied the line and retied it several times, carefully
demonstrating the twist that I spoke of, then handed her the
line. After a few unsuccessful attempts, I took her hand in
mine simply because I knew that I could. Touching her,
feeling how small her hand was, nearly made my hand
go limp. Letting go, she tried again on her own. When
she got it, her face erupted in joy.

"Ah! I did it!"

"Great. But believe me, you'll forget it if you don't
practice. And you have to practice from both sides of the
cleat because the other side feels totally different."

"I'll do it when Uncle Phillip isn't looking."

"You're Phillip's niece?"

"Yes, and I need him to think that I can do these
things." She coughed in her hand. She looked too delicate
to be on a fishing boat in the cold, damp weather of coastal
Alaska, and I imagined the weather affected her poorly.
"That's where the favor comes in."

"I thought that *was* the favor."

"That was part of it. If Phillip asks, can you tell
him that I already knew how to do this?"

"Sure. I'll even say that you gave me a few
pointers."

"Don't be funny, wise-guy. You have to make it sound believable." She stood and brushed the rope dust from her hands. "By the way, I'm Shenandoah, but everyone calls me Shenan," she said, pronouncing her name like Shannon. She extended her hand to me and I shook it without letting go.

"Like the song?"

"Yes. Everyone asks me that."

"I love that song."

"Do you play music?" she asked.

"I played the trumpet in high school."

"That's cool. I play guitar. I brought it with me."

I looked down at the boat under her feet and wondered where they found room to stow a guitar. A musical instrument was a strange thing to bring out on the Bay, but then again, a girl was even stranger. In those days, commercial fishing on boats with no bathrooms was very much a man's world. Certainly, the Native women who lived around the Bay fished a great deal, but I had never seen a non-Native girl on a boat before.

"You brought a guitar with you?"

"I sing to pass the time."

Shenan secured her hair against her windward ear, but the leeward side flew downwind like sea kelp in the ocean. The situation perplexed me. Here, in the middle of all these fishermen on the edge of Alaska, was a beautiful young woman whose self-professed skills were more musical than nautical. The situation was so unnatural, and her beauty so beguiling, that she may as well have been a mermaid.

She giggled and looked down at our hands. "Can I have my hand back?"

I let go.

"And aren't you forgetting something?" she asked. I looked down at the cleat, then back at her. "Your name?"

"Oh, I was trying to picture you singing on a boat and…" I shook her hand again, firmly this time. "My name is Jim. Jim LaBerg."

"Pleased to meet you, Jim," she said. "Aren't you cold without a shirt on?"

I let go of her hand. "No. Aren't you cold without shoes on?"

"Only a little."

"So, you're a puller on your uncle's boat?"

"What's a puller?"

"The person who pulls the net out of the water and removes the fish, but I guess that answers my question."

"Oh, I hope to be a puller. I asked Uncle Phillip if I could see Alaska with him. He said I could be his cook and deck hand. I guess we should have clarified what deck hand meant. I mainly cook for him and his other deck hand, Steve. But I desperately want to fish."

I was elated to hear she was a permanent member of the crew for I knew that Phillip and Joe fished together, and at nights their boats tied up together as they had now. Steve, Phillip's real puller, was an acquaintance of mine. We worked at a Bible camp together during my first summer in Alaska, before we landed the fishing jobs. I often thought that he was a poor fit for a Bible camp—all he wanted to do was drink and play cards and talk about girls. I was struck, then, by that last thought. Steve had to be relishing his new shipmate.

"Where is Steve?"

"He's in town, fetchin' some of our nets from the menders."

Fetchin'. There's a word I had never heard, or at least never heard like that. I detected a slight southern accent and asked her about it.

"What are you talking about? I don't have an accent."

"Okay."

"Where are *you* from?" she asked, deflecting the question.

"Washington. And you?"

"Richmond, Virginia. But my family is from the Shenandoah Valley, if you hadn't already guessed that."

"Ah, Poe's neck of the woods."

"Yes, are you a fan?"

"*I was a child and she was a child, in this kingdom by the sea, but we loved with a love that was more than love—I and my Annabel Lee.*"

"I'll take that as a yes."

"And you? What are you reading?" I asked, pointing to the book in her hand.

She looked at it like she had to find out for herself. "It's called *On the Road.* It's a book about this guy who travels around the country and just goes around doing different things for fun."

"A travel book?"

"Kind of that, and kind of a novel, I guess. It's really good. You can borrow it if you like. I've read it before."

"Thanks," I said. "I'll do that if I have time." I didn't tell her that the only book I brought with me was the Bible. I sensed she wouldn't think that was cool.

Phillip stood and yelled over the top of the pilot house. "You kids aren't getting into trouble, are you?"

Wanting to be alone with Shenan, I felt that these boats were too small. Onboard, no one was completely out of earshot unless they were in the small pilot house with its miniature kitchen or in the small berthing compartment under our feet. Phillip and Joe stepped carefully along the side of the pilot house and joined us on the bow. Phillip Harrison, the *Nereid*'s boat captain, was a short, square man with a mustache and bald head. "Jim, why did you crash our boats together?" he asked, pounding me on the back. "I don't want Shenan to learn how to do things the wrong way."

"I guess I wasn't paying attention."

"Something distracting you?" he said with a grin, elbowing Shenan in the ribs. I didn't answer. "I've got a serious question for you, Jim." He put his arm around Shenan's shoulders and gave her a friendly squeeze. "Was this Lady of the South much help in tying off? She claims she can do it all."

"Actually, yeah. If anything, I was in her way."

"Really?"

"Yep, before I knew it, she took the line out of my hand and tied off the cleat and said, 'If everyone around here moves as slowly as you, none of us are gonna catch any fish.'"

He tossed his head back and laughed. Shenan glanced at him, chuckling weakly, then looked at me and scowled.

"Good job, Shenan," he said. "But it looks like you might be catching more than fish out here."

"Oh, that's easy," she said. "I catch those wherever I go." She coughed into her hand again.

"Well, let's not catch too many fishermen or colds. I promised your parents I'd get you back in one piece." Then, turning to me, "Jim, I might need your help protecting Shenan's honor out here. You know how these roughneck fishermen are. My cook might be too much temptation for them."

He slapped Shenan on the shoulder and her face grew sour. "I'm not just a cook," she said. "I want to be a puller, too."

She was a fast learner.

"We can talk about that later."

She looked more upset. "And I don't need anyone defending my honor. The fishermen will just have to learn to control themselves. Real men don't objectify women. And besides, my honor is my own responsibility. Now, if you'll excuse me, I'm going to start dinner because that's what women do." She brushed by him and stormed toward the cabin.

Phillip waited till she was gone then jerked a thumb in her direction. "Her mother says she's fallen in with the hippie crowd." He looked toward the cabin. "But she has to cook. That was the agreement." He slapped me on the back and gave my shoulder a squeeze. "If you can figure her out, Jim, you let me know."

I had already figured a few things out. I understood that she was mad about being called a cook after proving herself with the cleat. Phillip was also quick to dismiss her comment about being a puller. But I couldn't understand why she would be upset about anyone defending her honor or what she meant when she said that cooking was a woman's job. There was so much that I didn't know back then. But I knew one thing for certain—she was different from any girl I had ever met, and I was dying to see her again.

## Chapter 2

# Youth Wasted on the Young

That night, we ate dinner on the *Nereid*. Without asking her, Phillip decided Shenan could cook for both boats. Soon, most of the meals would be salmon, but for now, it was spaghetti. It was too crowded in the cabin for more than three people, so we ate in the stern. It was a fine night. The blue-gray sky glowed over the treeless terrain of Bristol Bay. Long fingers of clouds reached down to the horizon touching their reflections in the glassy water. Other boats anchored around, tied together in groups of two or three. Like us, they waited for the season to start. The lights of the cannery and the city of Dillingham sprawled down from the hillside toward the water. My heart thrilled, not just at the thought of spending the evening with Shenan, but of spending many evenings with her. I was the luckiest man in the world—well, next to Steve, who got to spend all day with her and even slept in the same cabin with her. I wondered how Shenan felt about that.

While Shenan worked in the cabin, the rest of us sat on the fish holds toward the back of the boat. The two long boxes with lids ran across the boat and would eventually hold our fish, but for now served only as benches. Between them lay the picking area—the space between the two holds where fishermen pick fish from the net and where the net is stored when not in use. Joe, Phillip and Steve sat on the aft hold, while I sat just a few feet in front of them on the forward hold hoping Shenan would sit there as well. After some time, Shenan brought spaghetti on paper plates.

"Jim, this is yours," she said, stepping out of the cabin and onto the forward hold.

"Thank you." I noticed she found a solution to the wind, which had abated a good deal anyway. She wore a yellow bandana with blue polka dots around her head. She also wore shoes and socks. Standing on the holds, handing out plates of spaghetti, her thighs moved at my eye level and I felt a burn in my chest.

"Can you bring us some beers, Shenan?" Phillip asked.

Shenan dug her knuckles into her hips, almost elbowing my nose in the process. "I have to get your beer, too?" I was stunned that someone would talk to her boss like that, even if he was family.

Phillip, looking embarrassed, said, "I just figured that since you're cooking for us that—"

She returned her arms to her sides. "I'm sorry, Uncle Phillip. You're right—that's my job." She returned to the cabin.

I called after her, "I'll just take some water please."

"Is there anything else I can get you, sir?"

"No, that's all."

"That's right," Phillip said, "I forgot you don't drink, Jim."

"Well, I try not to."

"You don't drink. You don't party. You don't do women." He leaned back against the gunnel and scooped spaghetti into his mouth while he talked. "What they say is true—youth is wasted on the young. Why can't you be more like Steve? He knows a good thing when he sees it." He elbowed Steve in the ribs.

I felt another burn in my chest now, a different kind—pure jealousy. I wanted to be on this boat with Shenan. Steve looked at me smiling, bobbing his head up and down. He was not an unattractive guy, but nothing intelligent ever came out of his mouth, and I hoped Shenan judged his character the same way I did.

"Your parents put too much religion in you," Phillip said, concluding his thoughts.

Joe came to my rescue. "And yours didn't put enough in you." Joe, a Yup'ik Eskimo, was by this time an old man. His parents did not name him Nushagak Joe, of course. His real name was Joe Nukusuk, but the white fishermen like Phillip forgot his real name, so they called him Nushagak Joe after the river and the bay where they so often fished. Joe had the broad, round face of his people. Deep, weathered creases of his dark skin had petrified into a perpetual smile, which made him look always happy. A Russian Orthodox man, he possessed a good deal of wisdom, both practical and spiritual. He was also a very quiet person, so I was pleased to hear him come to my defense.

"Oh, Joe," Phillip said, "are you ever going to change?"

"I'm too old to change."

After handing out the drinks, Shenan got food for herself and sat down on the fish hold next to me with a plate and a beer. Like me, she sat with her back to the others. The two boat captains did most of the talking, mostly about where to fish—the Ugashik, the Nushagak, Egegik Point or some other place. It was the same speculation that all fishermen went through, trying to turn a game of chance into a science. I usually listened but didn't care one iota that night.

After sitting down, Shenan quietly whispered to me. "Thanks, by the way."

"For what?"

"For backing me up." Then, so quietly that I could barely hear it, "I think he actually believed it."

"About the cleat?"

"Yeah."

"Good," I said. I found myself watching Shenan scarf her food, her plate balanced nicely on her knees. She was of average height for a woman, certainly not tall. She was thin, but not a rail, and even with her baggy sweatshirt, I could tell that her chest was not large. When she reached across the hold to get another beer for Phillip, the sweatshirt lifted to her waist and I noticed she filled her corduroy pants quite well before her legs tapered into long well-formed calves. I remembered Shenan saying that real men didn't objectify women. In that sense, I had already let her down.

Shenan glanced at the cup of water in my hand and said, "Steve tells me you're a goody two-shoes."

I resented him for that. Oddly, I was even more upset that it was true. In the past, girls reinforced my strong morality, but I surmised that Shenan was far worldlier. In front of her, it just felt wrong.

"Well, that depends. I did lie to your uncle for you."

She took a drink. "That's true. But that was actually a very nice thing to do."

"Steve's just jealous."

"Do you know him well?"

"We used to work at a Bible Camp together."

"And?"

"We had a fight over some things he said about a girl."

"Ooh, sounds interesting. A girl you were dating?"

"In a way, I guess."

"What did he say?"

"He called her a tease."

"Was she?"

"Maybe."

"What happened with you and the girl?"

"We were interested in each other at camp, but the summer ended, and we all went back to college."

"You miss her?"

"She was nice, but it wasn't anything serious." What I didn't tell her was that I broke up with the girl when I discovered how many casual romances she had in the past, and I wondered whether Steve had been right. Besides, I didn't want to talk to Shenan about the past.

"So, you're from Richmond, huh?" I asked, changing the subject.

"Yes, but my family is originally from Harrisonburg. You ever been to Virginia?"

"No. I've never travelled anywhere except Washington and Alaska."

"That's not such a bad thing. If you're only going to visit one place, Alaska is the one—undisturbed wilderness, people living in tune with nature the way they did for thousands of years. It's such a mystical place."

I looked around me. There were no mountains close by—just vast sky and a tiny town in a thousand square miles of wilderness. And mud. Lots of mud capped by a green line of low brush. "Alaska is a wonderful place," I agreed, "but it's not much to look at here."

"Take my word for it," she said. "You'll travel more one day, and you'll see what I mean."

"When I do travel, that's one of the places I will go—to Virginia. I've always wanted to see the Jamestown Settlement, and the battlefields from the Revolution and the Civil War."

"We've got plenty of that," she said. "When you come, I'll show you around."

"I just might do that," I said, seriously mulling it over. I then asked, "What do you do?"

"I go to the University of Virginia."

"The one that Thomas Jefferson designed?"

"I'm impressed."

"I'm a history major at Washington State. What's your major?"

"General studies for now. I'm gonna be a sophomore and need to make up my mind." When she paused, I calculated that she must be eighteen or nineteen. "But I don't even know if I'll go back," she continued. "I don't necessarily want to do the whole nine-to-five thing. You know, live the American dream as it's fed to us by the people who dictate the norms of society. That's not me. I want to live how we're meant to live—in tune with nature, off the bounty of the land."

"Like a farmer?"

She smiled. "Maybe, but on one of the collective farms where people work to their ability and share their material goods."

I instantly realized that this girl was quite possibly a communist. I couldn't believe it—she seemed too nice to be a commie.

"And you? Why history? Do you want to become a historian?"

"No, I chose it because it's a good pre-law major."

"You want to be a lawyer?"

"I think so."

"That doesn't sound too convincing."

"Well, if I had my way, I'd probably study forestry or something that takes place in the outdoors."

"Why don't you have it your way?"

"No one is making me study one thing or another. I just feel that law would be a smarter career."

"It doesn't sound like you want to be a lawyer."

"No one really knows what they want to do until they actually do it, right? I'm the first one in my family to go to college, and I'm not going to waste it on some low-paying career."

"People should pursue their passions."

"Perhaps," I said, shrugging my shoulders.

"Have you been around Alaska much?" she asked.

"Not as much as I want to. I've been to Anchorage and the Kenai Peninsula. I drove to Fairbanks once. And I've obviously seen all around the Bible Camp, which is way up in the Matanuska Valley. I was a horse wrangler there and when I wasn't working, I got to explore the Talkeetna Mountains on horseback."

Her face lit up. "Wow! That must have been so out-of-this-world."

I chuckled. "It was out-of-this-world. I even worked a winter break and did some exploring then. It was cold, super cold, but I would go back in a minute. Sometimes I wish I went back to the camp instead of here. There's nothing in the world like riding those trails."

"Why didn't you?"

"Fishing pays much better. Plus, I get to see more of the state this way."

"Do you always choose the smart thing over the fun thing?"

"Everyone has to grow up."

"Those aren't the same thing. Besides, do you not like fishing?"

"I do. I've even thought about buying my own boat and fishing in the summers while practicing law the rest of the year."

"You think you'll settle here?"

"That's a strong possibility."

Shenan set her beer down, took a deep breath and proceeded to have a coughing fit into her hand. When it abated, I asked, "Did it go down the wrong pipe?"

She raised her index finger, asking for a minute, then coughed a few more times. Finally, she said, "You should probably know that I have asthma, and I think the cold air here makes it much worse."

"Are you going to be okay?"

"I'll be fine. I've had asthma fits my whole life."

"To be honest, I'm a bit surprised your uncle let you come out here."

"I think I know my limitations better than anyone." She sounded a little miffed. "I'll be fine, and I don't need anyone worrying about me. Just ignore my breathing fits." She exuded so much confidence that I took her instructions to heart and ignored most of her breathless episodes after that.

"I heard there's still homestead land in Alaska," she continued, "but that they're going to close it in a few years. Is that true?"

"Yes," I said, sliding back into conversation. "But the homestead land is way up north, not much good for farming."

"How do you know?"

"I've looked into it."

Shenan's eyes sparkled again. "That's so cool, Jim!" She said it so loud that Joe, Philip, and Steve paused momentarily before resuming their conversation. Then, a little more quietly, "You should do it. You'd be living the dream—getting your own land, living in the wild. I would give anything to do that."

I sensed this frail girl had no clue about Alaska, fishing, farming, homesteading, or even her own ability to deal with harsh weather. I made it my mission to give her an accurate sense of the world, or at least an accurate sense of Alaska.

"I don't think living with nature is as glamorous as you think. You would have to work all day just to stay alive. You would live in a rudimentary cabin with no plumbing. You would experience temperatures colder than you can even imagine. You would eat the same food over and over, and you would have to hunt for all of it. Do you know how to hunt?"

"No. Do you?"

"Yes, I grew up hunting."

"For trophies or for food?"

"Both."

"Hmm."

"What's *hmm* supposed to mean?"

"I think it's okay to hunt for food—even though a garden is much more energy efficient—but I find hunting for trophies deplorable."

"Why?"

"Because it's needless killing, and that kind of attitude will kill off all the animals in Alaska. This is one of the last untouched areas in America, Jim. In the world, I bet. Killing for trophies disrupts the cycle of life. That's not living *with* the land—that's conquering it."

I rubbed the stubble on my chin while formulating my response. "I think hunting *is* living with the land. The first time I hunted for deer, I felt more connected to the earth than I ever had before. It made me a part of the wilderness. And besides, you'd have to get real used to it if you lived in the bush of Alaska."

"What's the bush?"

"The backcountry."

"I was wondering what people meant by that. Anyway, I understand that hunting is necessary in the bush, and I don't want to be entirely judgmental, but I think trophy killing is wrong. Obviously, you have to hunt to live off the land. But can't you grow vegetables in Alaska?"

"Definitely. The cabbages in the Matanuska Valley are the biggest in the world. And you can grow carrots and potatoes. And some hay. Not Alfalfa, though. And, of course, the rivers are full of fish in the summer."

"And there are people doing this, right, living off the land?"

"Yeah, there are thousands of them—Natives and white people alike."

"That's what I want to do. I just don't know enough about it yet. That's one of the reasons I wanted to come to Alaska. Someday I want to live off the land."

"You'll have to hunt," I said, feeling amused.

"Or, I can have someone do it for me."

"No, you'll have to do it. What if the person you rely on is sick?"

"Then you'll have to teach me."

"Okay," I said, thinking that I would love to take her hunting. Looking at her, I tried to figure out if she was just a flake who would forget these notions at the first sign of adversity, or if she was a hopeless romantic who would die trying. Without warning, I imagined us living this life together. I pictured Shenan working in the garden and me hiking home with a load of caribou on my back, returning to a log home that we had built with our own hands. At night we'd light a fire in the stove after taking care of the horses. Then we'd join each other in bed.

This whole time she gazed at me with equal absent-mindedness till she caught herself and turned toward the others. "I better clean up this mess," she said in a tone loud enough for the others to hear. She picked up our things and stepped over the huge pile of net to collect the other plates. When she passed into the cabin, I felt something I'd never felt before—her absence—and I haven't shaken it since.

# Chapter 3

# New Ideas

Bristol Bay is a two-faced environment. It is not unusual for the tranquil seaside landscape to transform within a few hours to an angry gray blur striving in so many ways to kill you. The Bay is dotted with shoals and sandbars and is home to some of the highest tides in the world. When the tide is out, the shore is a twenty-foot wall of mud, making the land almost inaccessible. When the tide is in, however, you can see up over the land. It's possible for you to go to bed at night floating in a muddy ditch and wake up in the morning to a vista of rolling hills and swaying grass. When this happens, you must remind yourself that no one motored the boat to a new location while you slept. It's just that the tide turned, and the water lifted you to a higher plane of existence.

Such was the case that first night. The next morning, the tide had come in, and we woke up to the sight of the land around us. For lack of anything else to do, we sat on the fish holds mending our nets. Phillip and Steve did the same on the *Nereid*. Shenan was nowhere to be seen, presumably still in her rack. The sights and sounds of Dillingham, not far away, reminded us that we were still close to the last redoubt of civilization.

All our provisions had been purchased. The nets were in good shape and didn't need mending. We soon found ourselves splicing lines that didn't need splicing. Phillip and Joe were trying to avoid the bars in town, at least during the day. Every year, they set their minds to being good fishermen, focused and dedicated, but they both loved to drink. Phillip Harrison was also a womanizer. Shenan's Caucasian uncle fit in with the rowdy crowd in Dillingham and in his adopted town of Homer, Alaska where he lived during the winter. Rather than flying to the Bay, he used the *Nereid* in several different fisheries, and motored all the way from Homer. Middle-aged and divorced, he drifted like a ship without a rudder.

Nushagak Joe was a different man altogether, other than the drinking. He was quiet, religious and polite. Over the two seasons I fished with him, I gleaned that he kept dogs and a trapline in a town not far from Dillingham where he lived a modest life. But, like many of his extended family, he struggled with alcohol. It was unfortunate, then, that he became the unlikely friend of Phillip. Every year they found time to party. Phillip's temptation seemed to be the "snow bunnies," the Native women that a man could find without much effort, and Joe's was the alcohol. I had seen Joe stumbling drunk twice the season before, and I didn't want to see it again. Drunkenness drained him of all his admirable qualities.

Joe told me we needed supplies. I asked him what supplies. He couldn't name any, so I suspected they had debauchery on their minds. "You can come with us or go over to the *Nereid*." They were going to take our boat, the *Mikilak,* into town and leave the *Nereid* on her anchor.

"Who's 'we'?" I asked.

"Me and Phillip and Steve. Phillip's niece is stayin'. She's sleeping."

"I think I'll stay as well."

"That's what I would do." Joe smiled and turned to join the others. The boat rocked as he walked away. Phillip and Steve crossed over from the *Nereid*. I started to grab things that I would take to their boat. "Don't let them make you drink too much."

"Don't worry about me, young man. You need anything in town?"

"I could use some more razors and shaving cream and a bottle of aftershave if they have it."

Phillip laughed as he approached the cabin door. "What are you fishin' for, Jim? Fish, or something else?" Steve, who stood behind Phillip, laughed.

I shouldn't have asked for the shave kit within earshot of them, but my grooming plans had changed. I had intended to let my beard grow, but new circumstances had changed my thinking. "I forgot my shaving kit," I said, counting out a few bills for Joe. "That's all."

Joe pushed the start button, and the engine cranked to life. The other two moved to the corners of the boat to untie the two vessels.

"Last call, Jim," Phillip said. "We're leaving."

Open space appeared between the two boats. I hurriedly grabbed my backpack, stumbled out of the cabin, and jumped over to the *Nereid*. She rocked back and forth when I landed on the fish hold. As the *Mikilak* peeled away, Phillip waved and yelled, "Good luck for now, Jim! We'll get you some emergency cologne!"

"I didn't say cologne. I said aftershave! I just need to shave!" But it was too late—I had given them fodder.

When I thought about it, though, cologne was not a bad idea, and I hoped they would buy some.

As the *Mikilak* headed to town, I looked around for a comfortable place to sit. I spied into the berthing compartment, but it was covered by a hatch. It was nine o'clock and I wondered how long she would sleep.

I pulled my dog-eared Bible out of my bag, stretched out on the aft fish hold, rested my head on the small backpack and started to read. The sun beamed down, warming me. Slight waves rocked the boat. Seagulls screeched nearby. I fell asleep clutching the Bible to my chest.

Sometime later I woke to the sound of a particularly loud seagull. The sun had not moved far, and I figured I had slept less than an hour. I yawned and was disturbed by a female voice. "Good morning, sleepyhead."

I looked up, shielding my eyes from the sun. Shenan sat on the forward fish hold with her back against the gunnel. She wore shorts and her long, tan legs rested on the fish hold, stretching halfway across the boat. She wore the same bandana as the night before and clutched a blanket that was wrapped around her shoulders. I thought to myself that if she had worn pants she wouldn't need a blanket, but I wasn't about to complain.

I propped myself on my elbows and said, "Good morning. Though you're the one who's been doing all the sleeping."

"Is that so?"

"We got up at seven this morning, and when the guys left you were still asleep."

"Where did they go?"

"Town. They said they were going to the store, but I think they were mainly going to drink."

"Wow," Shenan said, "I didn't realize Uncle Phillip was such a partier till I came up here."

"Yeah, well…" I was trying very hard not to look at her legs, but they were so close.

"Why didn't you go?"

"I'm not really into that."

"Oh c'mon. You mean that a good-looking fisherman such as yourself doesn't have a lady friend in town?"

"No."

"Hmm," she said, skeptically. "I hear there's a lot of free-lovin' that goes on in town. Is that true?"

"Free-lovin'?"

"Yeah, you know what that is, right?"

"If you mean the kind you don't have to pay for, then unfortunately yes. There's plenty of both kinds in Dillingham."

"Why unfortunately? They say free love is the way of the future. It's not a bad thing."

I felt titillated and sick at the same time. "You don't think that's a bad thing?"

"Not necessarily. That's the way humankind was made, Jim. We're just another type of animal, you know."

My heart sank—from my chest to my gut. "I don't think that way."

"I don't mean the world has to be one big orgy. I just mean that society has trained us to think of love in a certain way, and there are so many ways in which it can be expressed. If a man and a woman like each other, they shouldn't be held back by the rules forced on us. You know—the rules set by economists and politicians who are just trying to maintain a baby-producing society."

Her ideas were disturbing to say the least. She was clearly from another world—a world I didn't like. I wouldn't have been surprised if her legs turned into a fish tail and she jumped overboard. She sounded more like a communist than the day before, and I regretted falling for her so quickly.

"Are you saying that marriage is just an institution created by… economists?"

"Not entirely." She sounded a little unsure. "There is definitely a place for marriage. Marriage is for two people who want to commit themselves to one another for the rest of their lives. I'm sure there will always be people who choose that path."

"Is that the path you choose?"

"I don't know." Her shoulders shrugged under her blanket wrap. "I'm only saying that we've been taught a warped view of sex, a lot of it done by preachers and Bible-thumpers," she said, gesturing toward the Bible on my chest. You know all this stuff we're seeing nowadays, like this war and aggression and people fighting one another—many people say that's a result of living closed, inhibited lives. We should stop inhibiting people— especially now that we have the pill. When people can't express themselves in natural ways, all that sexual angst gets transformed into aggression."

It was obvious now that this strange creature was advocating that people should be allowed to have sex with many different people, people they weren't even married to. These were not thoughts I had been exposed to. They were radically new. The year I met Shenan, 1969, was the beginning of the fracturing of the world, and the ways people thought and believed before that time and after that time changed in drastic ways forever. Shenan had been exposed to the new thoughts, while I had not. I could only frame her as the type of girl my mother had warned me about. The problem was that I had not expected wayward girls to look so beautiful or to sound so nice. Her demeanor felt wholesome and pleasant, but her words frustrated me so much that I felt like punching a hole in the boat. Maybe she was right about sexual angst leading to aggression.

"I'm not saying that marriage is wrong," she said, "I'm just saying that we have to think about the cultural norms that have been spoon-fed to us since we were babies. Not everything our parents taught us is right. And really, I'm not just talking about free love, because people get way too carried away with that. I, personally, wouldn't want to live like that." That comment, at least, lifted my heart slightly above my stomach. "I'm talking about people, and men and women, and families. Do you know what I'm saying?"

"Not really."

Shenan was very animated when she talked, and one thing I knew for certain was that it was refreshing to have a conversation with real meat. I had grown tired of talking about weather and fish and jobs and money.

"What I mean, Jim, is we need to look at our families. Like, why is it that the man gets to have a career while the woman is supposed to stay at home?"

"I guess because someone has to look after the children."

"Why do people have to have children?"

"They don't have to, I suppose, but I believe children are a blessing."

She waffled again. "I think children are a blessing, too, but not every woman wants that." Shenan thought for a moment before regaining momentum. "You see, I'm not saying that we *should* or *should not* do any of these things. I'm just saying that people, now, are starting to look at the way we do things and they wonder if everyone is supposed to live the same way."

"What you mean is that not everyone has to have children or get married?"

"Exactly."

"And that women should be able to pursue a career if they want to."

"Exactly!" She grew excited. Apparently growing warmer, she let the blanket drop from her shoulders. She wore a tank top with no bra, and the outline of her breasts imprinted clearly on her shirt. They were small, but well-formed and taut. Her sexual angst ideas now seemed correct with one major exception. I didn't feel like going off to start a war. In fact, I didn't want to go anywhere except to the next fish hold.

"It's possible," she said, "that a man and a woman can both work. Or even, that the wife could work, and the husband could watch the kids."

"I see where you're coming from, but a man can't nurse babies and—"

"And what?"

"And he obviously can't get pregnant, and getting pregnant would make it hard for a woman to work."

She exhaled sharply and dropped her shoulders. "Is that it—nursing and pregnancy?"

"Those are the only things I can think of."

"Thank God you don't say women aren't cut out for business or science or anything like that."

"No, I think women can be good at those things."

She smiled. "That is very mature of you to say, Jim. I'm proud of you." She coughed a few times, then shivered. Her body was not cut out for Alaska. "I have to admit that nursing and pregnancy are somewhat difficult issues, but they're certainly not insurmountable." Shenan turned her torso toward me to grab the blanket again, which tightened her thin shirt. "There's formula nowadays and women can bottle their milk." I felt light-headed. "And women can still work when they're pregnant except for perhaps a few months. We just need employers to be more flexible about that."

"That sounds reasonable."

"Then you admit that we need to change our society in some ways?"

"What?"

"Hello, Jim? Am I losing you?"

"No. I mean, yes. I think what you're saying sounds reasonable. I've seen families where I think the woman is much smarter than the man. And I know women who can work very hard—especially Native women."

Her eyes lit up. "You're a cool cat, ya' know that, Jim."

"I hope so."

"And there's so much more that needs changing."

"There is?"

"Yeees," she said. "Think about this. Why is it that black people in our society still live poorer than white people?"

"I don't know many black people." I tried to think of something intelligent to say. "But I've always wondered how things would have been different if Lincoln hadn't been assassinated."

She laughed. Leaning forward, she put her hand on my knee. "Jim, you talk real funny, but you are definitely one cool guy. I'm so glad you're not one of those people who think black people are inferior."

"The Bible says God is no respecter of persons. Black people are just as capable of doing great things."

"Oh, I know they are. One of my best friends, Desmond, is black and he's brilliant. He just graduated from Virginia with honors and he's starting medical school in Richmond next year."

"Wow, that's impressive."

There was a lull in our conversation. I could tell she was thinking about something as she looked over the water and I wondered if it was Desmond. I suddenly felt inadequate compared to her high-achieving friend. I looked at the book sitting beside her and tried to prod her into more conversation.

"Is that the same book?"

She picked it up and fanned through the pages. "No, I switched to a different one. This one is called *Never Cry Wolf*." She handed it to me. "I'm reading it for the third time. You'd probably love it since you're interested in biology."

"What's it about?"

"It's about a scientist who travels to Canada to study the wolves."

"Sounds right up my alley. Is it a true story?"

"Yep. He learns all about the wolves and becomes friends with them and discovers that they're not bloodthirsty killers."

"Hmm." I pondered it in my mind, for I was certain wolves were dangerous.

"Have you ever seen a wolf?" she asked.

"Once."

"Really?" Her hazel eyes widened. "I adore wolves. Where did you see it?"

"In a clearing by Castle Mountain."

"Where's that?"

"It's a long way from here, close to the Bible Camp."

"What did it do?"

"It looked at me a minute, then it turned and loped back into the forest and I never saw it again."

"That's so cool," she said. "I wish I'd been there. Are there wolves around here?"

I looked across the marsh meadows. A seagull cried plaintively from a lone piling near the shore. "I've heard people say that there are. There are wolves in most of Alaska, but the biggest packs probably live farther north where the caribou are."

"Are caribou the same as reindeer?"

"Pretty much, I think."

"He talks a lot about reindeer in the book. Are there many in Alaska?"

"If you mean caribou, then definitely yes. Hundreds of thousands. Maybe millions. You didn't see any when you flew out here?" I stopped myself. "Oh, that's right, you came in the boat. When I flew down here, I saw caribou herds that went on for miles." I stretched my arm out, painting a flat tundra landscape.

She looked like a child, wide-eyed and captivated. "Seriously?"

"Not exaggerating."

"How many?"

"Perhaps a thousand—maybe ten thousand."

"That is so amazing. I want to see that someday."

"Maybe you can. One of my dreams is to get a pilot's license so I can fly all over Alaska."

"You should totally do it."

"Have you ever been in a small plane?"

"No, but I would like to."

It was my turn to speak enthusiastically. "You should. Flying is pure freedom. It's just you and an engine strapped to some wings, and the whole world below you, and you can see everything from the air—all the animals, and the trees, boats and cars, and moose and bears, and tens of thousands of caribou."

"I would definitely fly with you."

"You'll have to wait a few years."

"Don't make me wait too long." After a short pause, she added, "Do you think there's a chance we might hear wolves while we're here?"

"I've never heard them."

"You know what I want to do?" she said as I handed the book back to her.

"What?"

"In this book, the scientist accidentally comes across the wolves when he's naked. He doesn't have time to put his clothes on and doesn't want to miss them, so he just runs after them."

She must have seen confusion on my face.

"Someday, I would like to run naked with the wolves, out in the wilderness, far from civilization. It would be so liberating, so powerful! Just to be out there with nothing but your natural body and the trees and the mountains and the wolves."

I must have looked at her like she was crazy, for her eyes met mine and turned away in embarrassment. She placed the book down again and wrapped the blanket tighter around her shoulders. She turned her head toward the low hills where she stared into the distance. Her hair moved in the breeze and I wondered about her. *Why would someone dream of running naked with wolves?*

Pieces came together—her book about a man traveling around the country, this book about wolves in the North. She was searching for that, for the things she read in books, and perhaps for herself. She was a little lost, I thought, and I determined to help her find her way.

I finally thought of something to say, but it wasn't brilliant. "I don't know if wolves would let you get that close." She didn't respond. "And it might be dangerous."

Tapping the cover of her book, she said, "This man did it."

"Well, scientists can be a little screwy sometimes."

She had no time for my misguided comments and turned toward the sun. I did the same, looking for whatever it was that she saw. I pictured myself running naked in the moonlight with wolves.

"But I suppose it would be exhilarating."

She turned toward me and smiled. "It would be like connecting with our ancestors. They lived like the wolves, you know, always moving with the herds, depending on them for everything."

"Maybe you want to do that because humans are very similar to wolves. I can see how that would be a spiritual moment."

"Probably similar to what flying is like for you."

"And possibly even better."

She smiled broadly. "Jim, I like you. I've never met a conservative who's so open-minded."

I felt that making her smile was my mission in life. No person had ever made me feel that way. "I have to be open-minded. I've never met anything like you in my life. I feel like *I'm* a scientist who's just discovered a new creature. It's like I'm studying you."

"I've noticed," she said with a vulpine look.

I didn't know how to respond. She reached one of her legs across the net that lay between us and placed her foot on the fish hold beside me. "They're just legs," she said. "Not much to learn there."

"I didn't mean… I meant I was learning things *from* you… from the things you were saying."

She removed her leg and returned it to the fish hold in front of her. She smiled, looking coy. "I know what you meant, Jim. I'm just teasing. You can study me. I think we can learn a lot from each other over the next six weeks."

"I hope so," I said. The thought thrilled me and scared me at the same time.

Chapter 4

# On the Bow of the *Mikilak*

Many of the things Shenan I talked about in 1969 came to pass. A few years later, I learned to fly, and it quickly became a central feature of my life. For thirty years I was a research biologist for the Alaska Department of Fish and Game. I studied most of the large mammals in the bush, most of them from the air. No one can estimate the populations of moose or musk oxen from an altitude of 200 feet like I can, and no one enjoys it more.

Shenan didn't lead me to become a pilot—that thought had already caught hold in my brain—but she set me on so many other paths. One of those paths ran alongside the wolves. I became an expert on wolves. And that is why it is odd that anyone would pay attention to anything I write about salmon. I am not a fish biologist. I am not the person to render an expert opinion on what the Pebble Mine would do to salmon. Still, people asked me about it, and this is what I wrote:

*While it is true that the Pebble Mine would sit at the headwaters of two major salmon rivers, we have no reason to believe that mines and salmon cannot coexist. One of the largest copper mines of all time, the Kennecott Mine near McCarthy, Alaska, produced more than a billion pounds of copper in the early twentieth century. Located in pristine wilderness at the headwaters of the Copper River, the mine's creation was fought over for many years. Conservationists lobbied Theodore Roosevelt's government, citing concerns that the mine, and the 200-mile railroad, would affect the river's millions of salmon and birds. They lost the argument. Both the mine and the railroad were built in 1909. The question is what has been left to us after the mine closed in 1938? A few scattered buildings deep in the wilderness, a rudimentary road that follows the old railroad grade. More importantly, it has left us a bird habitat that supports the world's largest populations of western sandpipers, dunlins, and trumpeter swans, and a thriving salmon run. The river is perhaps most famous for the fact that it is one of the few places on earth where a person can fish without a rod and reel. All you need is the net because the fish swim right into it.*

*As a biologist who has studied wildlife for decades, I have come to appreciate just how resilient wildlife can be. If done right, man and wildlife can coexist. There are coyotes and coywolves living in the backyards of cities on the East Coast. In 1989, the Exxon Valdez spilled 10 million gallons of oil in the ocean, but the exact effect it has had on the region's wildlife is hard to tease out now. In the Lusatia region of Germany, a vast area of coal-mining pits has been transformed into lakes and forests, and wolves have re-populated the area on their own, by swimming over from Poland. Alaskans can see something similar, on a much smaller scale, at the recreation area on top of the old Jonesville Coal Mine in Sutton.*

*The debates and courtroom battles being waged over the Pebble Mine are similar to the conflicts leading up to the Kennecott Mine in the early 1900's. And if you want to know what that mine did to the salmon, I suggest you take a trip to the massively powerful, murky waters of the Copper River. Bring a net with a long handle, dip it a few feet into the water, and wait. In a few minutes, you will have your answer.*

These are the words Finn Nickolai referred to—the words he said "meant so much." The words he felt opened the door for the Pebble Mine and set back his efforts to stop it. While I stand by the gist of what I wrote—man and nature can find ways to coexist—I have now seen something that has frightened me enough to give me a new perspective. And throughout all of this, I have heard the whispers of a ghost from the past.

*\*\*\**

Those initial conversations with Shenan were the first of many that summer. July came to Bristol Bay and the weather improved. The forlorn, desolate water transformed into a blue sea fringed by white bluffs, green shrubs, and purple grasses, which always moved, always undulated in the breeze. And, for brief intervals during the day, there was warmth. Shenan said that Bristol Bay on a warm day reminded her of the Eastern Shore on a cold one. It made me think that Virginia must be a perpetual Summerland.

As the days passed, we bobbed over the waves, plucking fish from the ocean. I felt alive, especially when interacting with Shenan. But more often than not, we fished out of sight from one another, and during those times I felt the Bay was a very lonely place. Bristol Bay may occasionally look like Virginia's Eastern Shore, but visitors might note the absence of quaint lighthouses, small villages, or much of anything at all. The Bay is nothing but miles and miles of marsh grass, ocean, and stunted vegetation. The Natives who control the land say the area is larger than the state of Ohio, yet only a few thousand souls can be counted there. It didn't help that Joe was so quiet. One day, I wondered aloud what Shenan was doing.

"Be careful with women, Jim," he said.

"Why?"

"Because they change you."

"In good ways or bad?"

"Both."

"What makes you say that?"

He shrugged his shoulders and said no more. That was typical of Joe. He said very little, but when he did, it was like he tried to compress a decade of experience into a single sentence.

Only one thing kept me and Joe from feeling utterly alone on the Bay—the floating city of gillnetters that congregated around the fish. The boats huddle against the invisible lines that the Alaska Department of Fish & Game calls legal fishing grounds. The boats weave like snakes over the water—each boat like an enormous head pulling a long body of net. Some snakes have bright red heads, others white, and still others a dusky gray. They writhe between each other jockeying for position. They compete to be the first net bombarded by a thousand silver missiles. You watch your net. You wait. You can't see the fish, but you see the signs. The floats jerk. They lurch downward when salmon hit the bottom. Splashes rise from salmon hitting the top. Occasionally, a tangled fish comes completely out of the water and spins back over the corkline. Before it gets too heavy, you pull the net over the roller and pick the fish from it one-by-one. Once the net is emptied, you throw it out again. This could last hours, or it could last days until Fish & Game puts a temporary hold on fishing. These closed periods are intended to permit millions of salmon to return to the exact same river where they were born so they can spawn and ensure the future of their species. I always wondered if the salmon remembered where they were born or if they were solely drawn by a place programmed into their DNA, a place that existed only in the distant recesses of their minds—their own heaven, their own dream, their own Summerland.

These closed periods led me to my own heaven. Nushagak Joe got on the radio and found Phillip and the *Nereid*. Nearly every other day, the two vessels rendezvoused in the mouth of some nameless creek a hundred miles from Dillingham, which was a thousand miles from nowhere. Many times, one of Phillip's fishing buddies tied up to the other side. Often, it was only the two boats.

Not more than a week into the season the *Mikilak* and the *Nereid* prepared to rendezvous. On approach, I saw Phillip and Steve in their slickers, looking very much like me and Joe. Shenan was not on deck. After a few small bumps, we tied off. I had seen Shenan and spoken with her two more times since those first days. She found me reading my Bible once and I told her at great length what I believed about God. She said that she had attended a church on special occasions growing up, but that it felt lifeless to her. I asked if she was a Christian, to which she replied that she was very "spiritual." She said she was open to religion, though. This gave me hope. Already,

I wondered if this woman could be a permanent part of my future, but first I had to shake her of her sacrilegious beliefs.

We took a break from eating salmon that night and enjoyed spaghetti again. Phillip gave permission to drink some of the Cokes as well. After filling our plates, Shenan asked Joe if she could eat on the bow of our boat. I knew that stepping over to a new boat was a relief after days cooped up on the same vessel. I asked if I could join her, thinking that was what she wanted, for moving to the other boat was the closest thing to privacy we could find.

Sitting down beside her with my back against the pilot house glass, I asked, "How's the cooking going?"

She shot a disgusted look in my direction. "What's that supposed to mean?"

"It's not supposed to mean anything."

"It's a sore subject right now."

I waited for her to continue.

"When I agreed to this job, I said I would cook, but I wanted to do other things as well. I asked if I could throw the net over the roller or pick some of the fish, but Uncle Phillip won't let me. He said it's too dangerous. I'm sick and tired of everyone feeling like they have to protect me. I asked him if I could hoist the anchor this morning and he said I could clean the cabin instead, and then we had an argument."

"What do you do all day?"

"Sleep and read the same books over and over, watch them fish, and cook. Mostly I just stare at the shore and wonder what the Alaskan wilderness is like."

The high bluff near us blocked the wind from our position and Shenan wore no bandana. In the sea-spray, her black hair had grown wavier than the first day I saw her. Even in the fading light, I could see that her skin was now a deeper tan, and I marveled at the fact that she appeared more beautiful every time I saw her.

"I'm gonna talk to him," I said. "You should be able to hoist the anchor or toss the net or even fish. I know Phillip. He's probably just worried about keeping you safe. If I had a niece on my boat, that's how I'd feel. But it makes no sense to have an extra set of hands sitting around doing nothing."

"You'd really do that?"

"Of course."

"When?"

"Wait here."

She turned her body toward me, crisscrossing her legs. "What are you gonna say?"

"I'm just gonna talk to him about it."

I walked the narrow deck between the two cabins, then crossed over to the *Nereid* where Phillip, Joe, and Steve ate on the fish holds. First, I went to the stove inside the cabin to give the impression I had merely come back for food, then sat down on the forward hold near Phillip.

They had been talking about fishing locations, but Phillip turned to me when I sat down. "You in the doghouse, Jim? What brings you over here with us boring men?"

"I'm not in the doghouse. I just wanted to ask you a question."

"Go on."

"Do you remember last year when Steve hadn't arrived in the Bay yet, and you needed help carrying your nets down from the menders?"

"Yes."

"After helping you, you said that you owed me."

He groaned. "What do you want? I'm gonna warn you that I can't make Shenan do anything she doesn't want to do." He laughed, and so did Steve.

I chuckled only to keep his good favor. "That's not what I was gonna ask, but it is about Shenan. She flew all the way across the continent because she wanted to learn to fish." He grimaced. "Or at least to help with fishing," I added, softening my stance.

"Just spit it out, Jim."

"I ask that you give Shenan a chance. Let her help. Let her operate the anchor windlass. I know she's not big, and she has asthma, but I'm pretty sure she can at least crank up the anchor. And I know it's dangerous, but that's what she wants. And when it's time to pick the net, she can at least throw the buoy over the side and sort the net when the fishing's done? That's not dangerous at all. And maybe she can pick a few fish."

He took a long gulp from his drink, then placed it on the hold beside him. Rubbing his chin as if he was in a lot of internal turmoil, he said, "Alright, Jim. So long as it's nothing dangerous. I'll have Steve show her a few things. But my agreement with her is that she does all the cooking and cleaning first. The deal's off if her first job gets neglected."

"She understands that. She has plenty of time to do both. If she does a good job, she could turn into a full-fledged fisherman."

"Don't get carried away, Jim. There's only five weeks left. Then he raised his voice and loudly proclaimed to the sky, "And she does have other jobs to do!" He turned and looked over his shoulder. Through the glass of the *Nereid*'s pilot house we saw Shenan's dark frame leaning around the edge of the *Mikilak*'s cabin.

In the faint light, her slightly obscured silhouette sat upright. Her voice loudly proclaimed, "I know!"

He chuckled, then growled to me, "Now get outta here and leave us boring men to our boring business."

"Thanks," I said, standing with my food.


I found that Shenan had returned to the spot in the center of the bow out of sight of the others. Sitting next to her, I said, "So, did you hear all of that or just the end?"

"All of it," she said. She turned toward me, resting her shoulder on the glass. Shenan pulled her ankles up beside her, pointing her knees toward me, and drew a strand of hair behind her ear. "Thank you, Jim."

"It was nothing."

"Yes, it was. It really means a lot to me."

I placed my not-yet-empty plate beside me and rested my hands behind my head. "Can I tell you something?"

"Sure."

"I had an interesting feeling today."

"Oh yeah," she said, pushing her clean plate away from her. The others talked and laughed far behind us in the *Nereid*'s stern.

"When we pulled up to the *Nereid* today, I saw you leaning against the cabin and I felt like you were still a stranger to me, and then… This is hard to explain. Then you turned to me and I felt that I'd seen you and talked to you a thousand times before."

Her eyes nearly twinkled, but she didn't say anything.

"And the revelation I had is… Well, I've always wondered how the salmon know how to get back to their birth-stream. And I just realized that this feeling might be what it's like for the salmon. That feeling of going somewhere that you don't remember but knowing you're in the right place when you get there."

"Jim," she said, playing with the edges of my flannel shirt, "I think you just experienced something that I was trying to explain to you the other night—about how life is a circle."

"How so?" I turned toward her.

She reached for my hand. She had obviously not done any fishing. Every part of her hand was soft and smooth. "I think life moves in a circle," she said, tracing the shape on my palm, "not in a straight line with a beginning and an end. Maybe you and I *have* sat together a thousand times before. I don't think people live just one life. You've heard of reincarnation, haven't you?"

I nodded.

"Buddhism and Hinduism teach us that we live and die and live again in a continuous cycle. Do you think that's possible?" She leaned her head against the pilot house, her eyes peering into mine. "Do you think that perhaps we have known each other before, perhaps in our most recent lives or a thousand lives before that?"

Her ideas clashed with everything I believed, but I was caught in her net and running out of struggle. "I don't know. I don't think so. I don't believe in reincarnation."

"What *do* you believe?"

"I believe that we have one life here on Earth and that if we serve God, he will reward us with everlasting life."

"That's such a narrow way of looking at things, don't you think?"

"What's so narrow about it?"

"That's just kind of sad—thinking that our only purpose is to follow the rules so we won't be punished."

"There's nothing wrong with that."

"If you think like that, you'll waste your whole life. We need to live life to its fullest, each moment, because life is all that we have. There may be nothing else. There may be no other world."

"If I'm reincarnated," I said, "then I'll have plenty of opportunities to do this stuff again. Besides, we shouldn't waste time trying to find heaven on earth. This life is but the blink of an eye, and it's the only life we have."

"That's why we should drink every drop out of it," she said, "I don't want to reach the end of my life and regret not having lived more."

"Well, neither do I."

"And if what you say is true, then what do you think of your revelation? Why do you feel like you've known me before?" A slight breeze spilled over the bank and Shenan leaned in closer until I could make out the details in her golden, animal-like eyes.

"I guess it's not because I have been here before, but because my ancestors have been here before. That's my revelation. I may be a human, but I have instincts, too."

Then she did something unexpected. She placed her hand on my cheek and gently kissed my lips. Her hair smelled of shampoo and sea salt and for a second I wondered if there truly might be heaven on earth. I wanted to kiss her more, but she pulled back.

"I'm sorry if you didn't want that," she said. "I got lost in the moment and your cologne and the stars and thinking about our genes and other people's lifetimes, and I just got swept away by it."

As she talked, I longed to smell her hair again. I could almost feel her hair running through my fingers and I wanted to kiss her neck. I wanted my mouth to run down her neck, to kiss the perfect line of the muscle running from the back of her head to the middle of her chest.

"Most men are animals," she said, "but I forget that you're different."

"I wish I could say that I was," I said, then placed my hand between her head and the glass and kissed her. I turned her head to expose her neck. My lips touched that spot where the muscle started behind her ear. It was a slow kiss for I lingered in the smell of the black waves, and then, just as I had pictured, I continued down the muscle toward her chest. Reaching the bottom, I went back up her neck to her chin until her lips were close to mine. I embraced her firmly and kissed her. I was there again in my strange, comfortable home, the place I had been longing for even though I had never been there before.

Just as we pressed our bodies fully toward each other, Phillip yelled, "Shenan, it's time to clean up!"

She leaned back and grimaced. "In a minute!" she yelled. We kissed again.

"Shenan!" he yelled a minute later.

She pulled back and said, "As much as I hate to say this, I'd better go. He's not gonna let me fish if I don't clean. You promised him that I would and he's testing us."

"I wish he could wait, though."

"I know," she said, "but we'll have more time. I promise."

She moved to stand. I stopped her for one last kiss. One kiss turned into several more. We were then interrupted by Steve, standing near us and leaning against the pilot house of the *Mikilak*. "Shenan, your uncle wants you."

After giving him a dirty look, she squeezed my hand and rose to her feet. She scowled at Steve as she brushed by him. Steve looked at me then walked away, but I didn't care what he thought. I laced my fingers behind my head and looked up at the stars. I had found the river in which I was meant to swim.

## Chapter 5

# The Cranberry Float

A week later, the fishing season hit full stride, and Joe and I scored big. Over and over we filled the fish holds to the top. A few times we had to quit in the middle of good fishing because the boat was full. Gently bumping against the sides of the cannery pier, I watched the cranes lift the bags called brailers away from our boat—each one a large sack of money. Joe and I did much better than the average boat. It was an exceptionally bad year for everyone else.

We had been fishing close to the *Nereid* all this time. I often saw Shenan on deck, but I never saw her fishing. She wore slickers like a fisherman, but only sat in the doorway of the pilothouse and watched. Sitting on an overturned milk crate, balancing her elbows on her knees, cradling her head, she watched the men work. Sometimes I caught her peering across the water in our direction. The image of us necking and kissing on the bow of the *Mikilak* ran through my mind almost continuously. When I saw her, my body ached to be close to her again.

After six days of solid fishing, we entered another closed period, which started in the early afternoon. We followed the *Nereid* into Egegik Bay. The tide sat low in the basin, the gray water a full fifteen feet from the grassy fields that thrived just above the high-tide level. Lying between the bluffs, these meadows of marsh grass filled the level plain like another fluid ocean of waving green. It was prettier and more alive than the water itself, enclosed by sandy bluffs topped with grass, dwarf shrubs and stunted trees. After days at sea, all land looked inviting.

As always, the *Nereid* dropped anchor for she was the bigger boat. In this, at least, I noted some progress. Shenan operating the windlass, carefully lowering the anchor to the bottom not far below. Phillip had clearly acquiesced to some degree. Once the anchor had taken hold on the bottom, we tied up. A boat called the *Lucky Linda* tied up to the starboard side. William "Wild Bill" Walmsley was the skipper. He had a large boat and two deck hands also from Washington. His guys, Rob and

Gavin, had befriended Steve when he first came to Bristol Bay the season before. Wild Bill, Rob, Gavin, Steve and Phillip all liked to play cards and drink. I always felt it was a shame that Joe had fallen in with them.

Shenan smiled as she came on deck. "Hello, Shenandoah," I said, calling her by her full name. I had done it once before and she told me that it was rare that anyone used her full name, but that she liked it when they did.

"Hello, James," she said, returning in kind. She pointed at the windlass. "Did you see that?"

"I did. You looked like a pro. Have you done much else?"

"Some. I've sorted the net and picked up loose fish."

"That's a start," I said.

"Thank you for intervening on my behalf."

"You deserve it."

She smiled at me, then looked out toward the bluff. "It's beautiful out here," she said, shielding her eyes. "You think we can go ashore?"

"If Joe and Phillip say it's okay."

"How do we get there?"

"We run and jump, and hope the ground isn't too muddy."

Both Joe and Phillip approved of our plan if we promised to stay close and not be gone too long. We finished a few chores and packed bags with lunch and books. I waited for Shenan on the *Mikilak* as it was closest to shore. The other guys had already collected in Phillip's pilothouse with cards and a bottle of whiskey. Gavin and Rob had been eyeballing Shenan since they came aboard, watching her move about in sweatshirt, shorts, and bandana. Steve rolled his eyes when he heard our plans. "You better hope they don't open the fishing while you guys are out screwin' around," he said before taking a shot of whiskey. He turned back to his cards as Shenan and I left the cabin.

Shenan turned and walked toward the bow, her hips cocked to the side, balancing one hand on the pilothouse.

"I see you're wearing boots with shorts now," I said. "That's a sure sign you're turning into an Alaskan." She glanced over her shoulder and smiled. She looped one leg toward me and wiggled the boot playfully. "You like 'em?"

"Very much, but I hope you brought warmer clothes."

She squeezed the bag in her hand. "I've learned enough about Alaska to know you should always bring more clothes."

After following her to the bow, I made a running leap onto the tidal mud. My feet sunk only an inch, leaving a mildly wet depression in the sand. Shenan tossed our bags to me, then ran and jumped. She didn't make it past the wet part. On landing, one boot stuck in the mud. She plunged forward onto her hands and knees. We laughed as she crawled back to the boot a few feet behind her trying to keep her sock clean. She pulled it out of the clay with a popping sound and put it back on. After helping her to her feet, we donned our backpacks and set off toward the bluffs. Along the way, I scanned the ground.

"What are you looking for?" Shenan asked. I bent over to pick up a shiny object. It was just a wet rock, so I tossed it aside.

"Glass floats."

"Floats?"

"You know the Styrofoam floats on the tops of our nets—the corks?" She nodded. "Well, back in the old days, they used to make floats out of glass instead of Styrofoam. They come in different colors, but they're usually green."

"Do you collect them?"

"I've only found one. I like them because they're like a piece of history. They get lost in the ocean for decades. It's like finding a time capsule that's traveled thousands of miles. They say most of them are from Japanese boats."

Shenan scanned the ground with me, but we reached the edge of the bluff without finding a thing. Climbing to the top, we set off through the high grass, still with no destination in mind.

"The guys keep talking about how you and Joe are catching all the fish."

"Oh yeah?"

"Yeah, we're not doing so well, I guess."

"I know. It's a down season for a lot of boats."

As we walked, the dry stalks scratched our legs and a plethora of mosquitoes and gnats swarmed us. The insects almost made me long for the water again. I broke off a stalk of grass and rolled it in my teeth.

"I don't understand how it can be so different," she said, "when we're fishing the same spot as y'all." I had gotten used to the word "y'all" by now, though it didn't escape her lips often. The first time I mentioned it to her, she denied saying it.

"Well," I said, watching the ground ahead of me, "do you really want to know what I think about that?"

"Of course."

"You see, both Joe and I are praying men. We pray together that God will bring us a bountiful harvest."

"That's kind of creepy," she said playfully. "Do you guys hold hands when you pray?"

"No."

"I'm glad to hear that," she said, making us both chuckle at the image.

"Ouch!" Shenan slapped a mosquito on her leg. It was much warmer the farther we got from the water. "Do you think God would actually take the time to look after two fishermen like that?"

"I know that he would."

"How do you know?"

"It says so in John 21. Jesus told the disciples to cast their net on the other side and they caught so many fish they couldn't haul the net in."

"You really believe that, don't you?" she said, her breath winded.

"Yeah."

"Well, if you and Joe continue to catch fish like you have, maybe I'll believe it, too."

I honestly believed at the time that Joe and I would continue catching more fish than anyone else. I believed my prayers moved mountains and oceans. I also believed that Shenan would come around to my way of thinking. I believed in a lot of things back then.

"Oww!" she said again. Shenan stopped this time and examined the blood from the mosquito she had just killed. "We've got to get out of these weeds." Then, she bent over resting her hands on her knees.

"Are you okay?"

"I'm fine. It's just my asthma." She started coughing, like something had caught in her throat. I scanned the horizon, sensing immediately how far we were from help.

"Do you need anything?"

"My backpack," she said, still bent over.

I helped her wiggle it off her back and placed it on the ground in front of her. Rummaging through its contents, she retrieved a small glass bottle with a white tube on it, placed her lips on it and sucked in.

"What's that?" Still bent over coughing, she held her finger out asking for a minute. "Never mind. Don't talk," I said, rubbing her back, "just breathe."

A minute later, she caught her breath and said, "An inhaler."

"Medicine?"

"Yes."

I realized I shouldn't make her talk and waited a minute more. She eventually stopped coughing and regained her breath. Finally, she stood up with her hands on her hips.

"You sure you're okay?"

"I am now."

"Maybe we should get you to a doctor."

"I've already been to a doctor. That's why I have medicine. Don't worry—this is normal for me." She smacked another mosquito on her leg. "But these bugs are killing me."

I pointed to an earthen dam I had seen earlier. "Let's go over there" I said. "There might be a pond behind it."

"Let's go," she said, striding in that direction.

Two minutes later we stood on the dam looking at the small blue pond. Apparently, it had been the source of water for an old cannery. One lone pipe protruded from the dirt and a steady current of water poured to a puddle below. From that vantage point, Shenan and I saw far out onto Bristol Bay and its small host of fishing vessels near the shoreline.

"I'm going down," Shenan said.

"Down where?"

"To the pipe. I'm hot and muddy and stinging all over." She ran around to the pool and removed her boots, sweatshirt, and bandana. Her black hair was now as tangled as the weeds around us. She dipped her long leg into the pool, feeling the bottom. "Ooh, it's muddy," she said. "Are you coming?"

I walked across the dam to reach her. By the time I approached the pool she was already showering under a smooth, heavy stream of pond water. It poured over her forehead, all over her tank top and shorts, and down her scratched, mosquito-bitten legs. I removed everything but my jeans and stepped into the pool.

She motioned for me to join her under the stream. The cold water hit me like a bolt, nearly taking my breath away. But it brought relief to my itching arms and sweating back. Shenan embraced me under the heavy stream and tucked her head under my chin. She trembled.

"Are you cold?"

"I'm freezing," she said, her voice trembling.

I laughed. It's almost seventy degrees out here."

"I know, but the water's cold."

"Isn't that what you wanted?"

"Not *this* cold."

"Do you want to get out?"

"Not yet."

We stood there a few minutes more. I wrapped her firmly in my arms and held her head against my neck. She shivered.

"Okay, let's go."

I held her hand and helped her out of the pool. She looked rather skinny now with her tank top wedded to her small breasts. Even her hair seemed small without its waves and curls. "Here, put this back on," I said, grabbing her sweatshirt from her bag and wrapping it around her shoulders. "Let's sit over there." I pointed to a knoll covered in short grass beside the pond.

We walked together, her teeth chattering, her fists tucked under her chin, and my arm tight around her, resting comfortably on the slope of her hips.

Reaching the spot, we sat on thick, springy moss. It was refreshingly warm. Sitting behind her, I sheltered her with my arms and legs. I pulled her hair away from her back and used the sweatshirt to dry it as best I could. Putting my arms around her, I held her tight and rubbed the sweatshirt against her skin. There was a gentle breeze high above the pond, and though it didn't help to warm her, it kept the mosquitoes away. She pulled a brush out of her bag and handed it to me. I started brushing my hair.

She turned and laughed. "I meant for you to brush *my* hair—before it dries." She sat quietly while I tentatively worked the brush through her wet, gnarled hair. At first unsure of myself, I quickly determined it was not very different than brushing a horse's tail.

"What should we talk about?" she said.

"Tell me something about you." I paused from brushing her hair. "How did you get the name Shenandoah?"

"I was named after the river, and the stars."

"The stars?"

"That's what Shenandoah means—the Daughter of the Stars." She cleared her throat. "A long time ago a tribe of Natives lived in Virginia. This was before they were driven out by the white man. They called themselves the Shenandoah after their river. According to an ancient legend, after the Great Spirit made the world, all the morning stars gathered for a council at a beautiful spot—on the shores of a shimmering lake in the midst of tall, snowy mountains.

"They went to this same place every time they had a meeting. They hovered over the lake and flew across the waters. Their lights flashed on the mountain peaks and reflected off the lake. The lake was the place where they sang songs of joy and fellowshipped together and made important decisions.

"Every thousand years, the morning-stars gathered in this spot to conduct their meetings, to sing their songs, and to shine their colors over the snowy arena. But as all things change, so too did their world. During one of their absences, the natural dam broke apart and tumbled to the valley below. The lake drained and disappeared.

"Over the course of many years, it was time for the stars to return, but they could not find the mighty arena they remembered. After years of sad searching they gave up and looked for a new place. Looking far and wide, they found another valley, but this one had a river instead of a lake, and rounded, blue mountains instead of snow-capped peaks. Still, it was beautiful. This valley was old and graceful like them. They flew around and found that small features looked familiar. Soon, they realized that this was their old valley, worn away by the seasons of time. They rejoiced at finding their meeting-place, and marveled at its new look, just as beautiful as it had been in ancient times, but in a different way. To commemorate it, the stars removed the brightest jewels from their crowns, and placed them into the river where they shine and sparkle to this day. And that is why the Natives who lived there long ago named the river, Shenandoah, which means Daughter of the Stars."

"That's beautiful," I said, realizing I had been so caught up in the story that I stopped brushing her hair. I resumed with the strand still in my hand.

"I like to think so. I've always been proud of my name. Now tell me something about you."

"What do you want to know?"

"If you settle in Alaska, what kind of house do you think you'll have?"

"Some sort of log cabin, I suppose."

"I thought you would say that. A small one?"

"Probably, at first. But eventually I'd like to build a large log home. Probably two stories with one wide eave coming off the front."

"Wait," Shenan said, reaching for her backpack. She pulled out her copy of *Never Cry Wolf* and a pencil, then handed them to me."

"What's this?"

She opened it to the inside cover. "Draw it here."

"In your book?"

"Yeah."

"I don't want to ruin it."

"You won't ruin it. I like personalized books." She took the brush from me, turned to face me, and brushed her own hair. "It will give the book personality."

I sketched the log home inside her book, then added a stream and trees.

"It's beautiful. How do you get over the stream?"

"Perhaps I'll build a bridge."

"That would be pretty." She took the pencil and the book and sketched an arched bridge with an ornate railing over the water, though I had pictured flat logs with planks.

"Don't you think you would have horses?"

"Of course."

And on it went like that until she had drawn horses, a horse barn and a garden. At her request I drew mountains behind it. She capped it off with a tire swing in the yard for the little "blessings" that I said I wanted. She said that was necessary because the whole place couldn't be about work, and kids always love tire swings.

We admired the finished drawing. She leaned back in my arms and craned her neck to look at me. "You think that will actually happen, Jim?"

"What?"

"You think you'll settle in Alaska and you'll be able to build all those things?"

"I don't know. It will take a long time. I have to finish college and start my law career and lots of other things."

"You're not going to be a lawyer."

"Oh yeah?" I said, chuckling. "Then what am I going to be?"

"You're going to be a bush pilot."

"Is that so?"

"Yes, you're going to do it because you're passionate about flying and the wilderness. And you're not even interested in the law."

"But I'd be poor."

"That's okay. You don't need money. You could build your own cabin, and you won't need running water or electricity."

"You know me that well, huh?"

"No, I just know that mankind got along without those things for thousands of years, and you strike me as the kind of guy that could do without them."

"True, but I haven't found too many women who would be willing to do the same."

"I would."

"You think you could do without a hair dryer and a TV?"

"Ah!" She turned momentarily, looking disgusted. She turned around and sat on my lap, straddling my torso and resting her arms on my shoulders. "You don't know me, Jim LaBerg. I don't need those things. I'm on a boat peeing in a bucket for goodness sake! You think I couldn't do without electricity?"

"Good point." I backed down because my mind had been set on one thing all day—necking with her like we had on the bow of the *Mikilak*—and I couldn't do that if I made her mad. "You're right. You're tougher than the girls I've met before." I chuckled and her smile returned as quickly as it disappeared.

As if propelled by the wind at her back, her body leaned into mine and she kissed me. She was capricious as the wind—one moment hard and cold, then shifting in a moment, to warm and gentle. I couldn't get my mind around her. She was intellect versus instinct. She was either everything good and wholesome, or she was sin. I didn't know that it was perfectly reasonable to be both. I wrapped my arms around her and pulled her closer, feeling her belly against mine, her breasts against my chest. I felt where this moment was leading, and I wanted to go there with every fiber of my being. Yet, everything I had ever been taught told me that it was wrong—that I would be taking advantage of her, ruining her, and giving in to sin. Things were different back then. After kissing for several minutes, I stopped.

"Jim," she said, her eyes closed, her lips reaching for mine.

"Shenan, not now."

"Why?"

"I don't know. I won't be able to control myself."

"Why?" She tried to kiss me again.

"I don't want it to be like this. We have to wait till we're married."

She jerked her head back and opened her eyes. There was nothing in the world but me and her and the wind at her back. A smile played on the corners of her lips. "What makes you think I'd ever marry a guy like you?"

"I meant *if* we were married."

"And then, every night for the rest of our lives?" she added with a devilish grin.

"Exactly."

"Well, don't worry about it, Jim LaBerg, because the only man I'm going to marry is going to be a free spirit, filled with passion about his work, and not a slave to a career he doesn't love."

"And he's going to have a log cabin," I added.

"And that, too."

"And no electricity."

"Electricity is optional, but he'd have to be a happy man, doing what he loved."

"Is that all?"

"And he'd have to realize that even if we weren't married, we could kiss as much as we wanted, and he'd have to know that there was nothing wrong with that."

She was right, and my body ached for excuses. I slid one hand around her waist and laid her on the mossy ground. Pulling her body close to mine, I dismissed any feelings of guilt. She was right—it was only kissing.

At some point, prompted by I know not what, we gathered our things to return to the boats.

For ten minutes or so, we marched through the brush, paying little attention to the weeds and scratches. The weeds gave way to tall grass as we approached the bluffs near the inlet. The tide was low, and we descended the steep embankment and walked along the silty beach toward the inlet where the boats waited. I was in the middle of describing to Shenan how people live in the bush with no electricity when I heard her voice call out from behind me.

"Jim."

I turned to find her ten paces behind with her hands behind her back. She wore a broad smile. "I have something for you." Bringing her hands to the front, she produced something about the size of a small apple. Though partially covered in silt, I could see that it was a net float made of cranberry-colored glass.

"A red one." I took a few steps toward her. "These are super rare." As I reached to touch it, she jerked it back and returned both hands behind her back. My hand froze over the spot where the float had been.

"You can have it, for a price." My hand returned to my side. "It will cost you one kiss."

Placing my hands on her hips, I teased her with just a peck on the lips. Before I pulled away, she bit my lower lip, letting it slide slowly between her teeth as I pulled back. Pain and excitement coursed through my body. I touched the painful area and found a dot of blood on my finger. "Sometimes I swear you were raised by wolves."

"Sometimes I wish that I were," she said, slipping the cool glass into my hand. "You earned this."

Still palpating my lip, I held the float up in the sunlight. A tiny puddle of water rested inside the glass. I sloshed it around. "Where did you find this?"

"Right there." She pointed to a round hole in the gray silt. "It was the universe speaking to us."

"I didn't know the universe could talk."

"Oh, it can," she said, slipping her hand into mine, "if you learn how to listen."

After dinner, we parted ways. That night, I tossed and turned, lost in vivid dreams of her eyes, her neck, waves of green marsh grass, and waves of long black hair. I was in a small rowboat and she came up from the ocean—cold, wet, and naked—and leaned her elbows on the side of my boat. She reached into the sea and produced the red float. I tried to take it, but she held it in her grip. Our hands remained locked together. We kissed, and she shivered when we kissed, and we kissed until the stars came out. Her watery eyes reflected the stars above. Without warning, she placed the float in my hand, and her eyes turned black and she dove into the ocean with a splash. I awoke at this point, cold and lonely, then remembered she was sleeping peacefully in the boat next to mine. Comforted by reality, I thought of her and the darkness of the dream dissipated.  More than forty years later, I still have this dream, but she is no longer near me, and the darkness lingers.

# Chapter 6

# Overboard

Two nights after Shenan gave me the cranberry-colored float, things started to go bad. In the middle of the night, Nushagak Joe stumbled back to the boat after a night of drinking on the *Lucky Linda*. From what I could tell, Joe's leg fell between the two boats and his forearm came down on the gunnel as he tried to break his fall. He saved himself from falling into the water, but I heard thumping sounds on the wooden hull and Joe's cry of pain. I found him hanging between the two boats, struggling to get onto the *Mikilak* as he hung precariously over the frigid water below. As I hoisted him over the gunnel, he winced while cradling his left arm.

Phillip and Steve responded to the ruckus and the three of us laid him on the fish hold. His left forearm bent unnaturally, but that was his only serious injury. Shenan, apparently in a deep sleep, never came on deck. Leaving Phillip with his boat, Steve, Joe and I shoved off in the *Mikilak* and headed toward the hospital in Dillingham. After my dream, I was half-tempted to ask Steve if he had laid eyes on Shenan—if she had indeed retained her human form and remained in the world of us landlubbers. Of course, it was all nonsense.

The doctor said Joe fractured his arm and needed a cast. Joe refused, but the doctor would hear none of it. We pinned him down for the procedure. The doctor worried aloud that this stubborn old man would cut the cast off the next day. I assured him that Joe would leave it alone once he sobered up. Seeing him drunk and combative saddened me—that wasn't the real Joe.

Steve caught a ride back to the *Nereid* while I stayed the night with Joe in the hospital. Unable to sleep on the sterile sheets stretched over the hospital bed, my thoughts turned to the whirlwind of events I had experienced the past three weeks. I could see how quickly my feelings had grown toward Shenan and, for the first time, I doubted them. With distance between us, and in a sleep-deprived state, I took a sober look at our relationship. We were very different people. Was there any chance we would see eye-to-eye on religion, worldviews, or politics? Most likely, we would spend our whole lives fighting once the initial attraction wore off. Still, I held out hope that I might bring her round to my way of thinking.

I thought, too, of the fishing season. The *Mikilak's* prospects had dimmed, and I wondered if it was a sign. As Shenan would say, the universe was speaking to us. We had stepped out of God's will and were now paying for it. I told Joe as much on our walk down to the harbor. I tried to remind him of the evils of alcohol. He did not reply. I told him that I determined to think more clear-headed around Shenan. I had not determined to end the relationship, but to take it slowly and to keep my wits around her. I know Joe was capable of good advice, but he offered none. In retrospect, I see that it was because I didn't ask for it. I also see that he hadn't asked for mine.

The next day, Joe and I scratched the water for fish. He was in pain. The fishing was spotty and pulling the net alone was hard work. Joe covered his cast with a piece of plastic and tried to pull with one arm, but his contributions were mostly symbolic. We caught no more than thirty fish that day, and even that was difficult. Joe said that if the net were full, we'd have a hard time getting it in the boat before it was completely plugged, and that would spell disaster. We didn't talk about quitting, but it was on our minds. Both tired and defeated, we pulled alongside the *Nereid* when the fishing period closed in the middle of the afternoon.

We sat in the middle of the floating city with no land close by, and no chance for escape. Like most days at sea, the two boats comprised our entire world— small, confining, and unbearably familiar. The seagulls screeched endlessly over our heads, mocking us with their unfettered mobility. I hadn't been to a barber in weeks and my hair had grown long and curly. Stretching my legs on the near-empty fish hold, I picked at the dried fish scales on my face, neck and arms that felt like so many scabs. Shenan stepped over. My heart thrilled. My heart sank. I was tired and torn.

Working on some hidden scales behind my elbow, I noticed how tan I had become, but when one of Shenan's legs descended onto the *Mikilak* I noticed the sun had favored her more. I don't know how she managed to wear shorts in the cool Alaskan summer, but she did. With her black hair in two long braids, she looked almost as Native as Nushagak Joe.

"Hello, Pocahontas," I said, brushing the now loose scales from my body. I smiled despite myself.

"I am part Cherokee, you know."

"Doesn't everyone in America say that?"

"I actually am. My great grandparents were both full-blood Cherokee."

"That makes you . . . one-quarter?"

"I never met them, but I wish I would have. My mother never talks about that side of the family. She's embarrassed about it even though I think it's something to celebrate."

Shenan sat on the fish hold facing me, her legs straddling either side. She was smiling, beaming, and beautiful. The blood of her Native ancestors expressed itself in her features. She inched closer to me, but I refused to put my legs down. I feared that if I didn't block her, I would be unable to resist her charms.

"That's terrible about Joe," she said. "His face is really bruised up." I could see that she mistook my moroseness as a reflection of what had happened to Joe.

"The worst part is how it happened," I said. "He tries so hard not to drink, but whenever he gets around other drinkers, he can't help it."

"I don't think he tries very hard."

I shrugged my shoulders.

"Are you guys still gonna fish?"

"Yeah. Why do you ask?"

"I heard Joe talking to Uncle Phillip about it just now. He said you guys were going to have a tough time."

"We'll make it through."

"I missed you," she said.

"I missed you, too." I was unsure of the direction of our conversation. Several seconds passed before I found something to say. "Have you done any fishing?"

Her shoulders dropped. "No. All I do is cook and clean and hoist the anchor."

"He won't give in, huh?"

"I know that he never said that I could fish, but I just assumed that he would let me, especially after you talked to him."

"Are you still doing your chores?"

"Yes," she said, though she seemed put off by my question. "I do what I'm required to do, but I won't clean up after Steve. That guy is a pig, and I'm not going to clean up their personal stuff."

"Well, if Phillip doesn't think you're keeping your end of the bargain, then of course he's not going to keep his end."

"I just don't think it's right that I'm relegated to the cleaning just because I'm a woman."

"That's irrelevant. That's the job you were hired to do and that's the bargain we struck with him."

She pursed her lips and looked at me as though she wanted to say more. "Perhaps."

"It's more than perhaps—it's pretty straightforward."

She shrugged her shoulders. "Regardless, it looks like I won't be fishing this summer."

I was miffed to discover that she dismissed the bargain but was in no mood to press the issue. "I guess your summer experience isn't quite what you'd planned," I said.

She leaned back, placing her hands behind her. "No, but it's been more than I hoped for in other ways."

"You plan to come back next summer?"

"I don't know. A year is a long way away. No one even knows if they'll even be alive in a year."

"That's morbid."

"But it's true. Besides, I'd have to be invited back, and at the rate I'm going I don't think I will be."

"Perhaps you can work on my boat."

"This one?"

"No. I'm thinking about buying my own boat." I was surprised to hear the words coming out of my own mouth.

She leaned forward again. "Really?"

I cocked my head to the side, not sure if I wanted to share my plans. "I saw a used boat for sale yesterday, and I might have enough money for a down payment after this season."

"That's so exciting!"

"It's fairly new—a fiberglass type. There's a boat on the water that looks a lot like it."

"Which one?" she asked.

I rose to my feet and stood on top of the fish hold. Shenan stood next to me. Scanning the fleet of boats all huddled in groups of two or three, I found the one I was looking for. "That one. Except the one for sale is kind of a salmon color."

"That's fitting." She took my hand and braided her fingers through mine as we stood precariously high on the fish hold, the boat rocking gently beneath our feet.

"Do you think you'll get it?"

"Jesus said that if we have the faith of a mustard seed, we can move mountains."

"I bet it's pretty, Jim."

"She is."

She played with my fingers for several seconds. "It's funny how men always call boats *she*. Do you think of boats like women?"

"Maybe. Perhaps I should be bothered by the fact that another man had her first."

I laughed. She didn't.

"Is it important that both your women and boats be virgins?"

I felt bile rise in my throat. "I can probably make exceptions for boats."

Another pause. "Then it's probably good you're only asking me to be puller?"

My emotions went flat. We stood there for several awkward seconds. Holding her hand now felt anything but natural.

She tried to change the subject. "Don't you think it's cool that both Jesus and the Buddha have parables about mustard seeds?"

"I didn't know they did."

"Do you want to hear it?"

I grunted.

"It goes like this. An old lady whose husband recently died came to the Buddha for help with her grief.

He said he could help her, but that first she would have to go into town and ask for mustard seed. The only condition was that the seed had to come from a home that had not experienced loss. She went door to door, but everywhere she went she heard stories of grief. By the time she returned to the Buddha, she learned that loss was a part of every person's life."

"And?"

"And that's it. That was the lesson he wanted her to learn."

"That's kind of depressing, don't you think?"

"But it's true, isn't it?"

"I don't know. That's the difference between your god and mine. My God says if we have faith, we can prevent suffering, and your god says that we just have to learn to accept it as a part of life."

Shenan furrowed her brow. "First of all, the Buddha is not my god—"

"Are you a Buddhist?"

"I don't think so, but if I was, would you not let me be a puller on your boat?"

"I don't know if I'd have you be a puller on my boat anyway."

Her eyes scanned my face. "Then what would I do on your not-so-virgin boat?"

I didn't know the answer to that question. The night before, in the hospital, I told myself that a future with her was unwise, and our conversation today was proving it. But for some reason I told her about the boat when I had only briefly considered buying it. Perhaps I had meant that she would be a puller. I didn't know. When I was near her, my mind gravitated toward notions like that—notions of living with her. It was obvious I had no control over my own thoughts when I was around her, and our current conversation convinced me of my error.

"I don't know what I meant. It probably wouldn't be a good idea."

"Why wouldn't it?"

"Shenan!" Phillip's voice boomed from the cabin of the *Nereid*.

"Yes, Uncle Phillip?" she yelled in response, sounding annoyed.

"When you get a second, we need to talk."

She pursed her lips, then turned and yelled over her shoulder, "I'll be over in a minute!" She returned her attention to me. "Why wouldn't it be a good idea?"

"Because of us."

"What about us?"

Sleep-deprived and frustrated, I knew this wasn't the best time to talk about it, but I thought I might as well get it out. I cleared my throat and looked at the sea to avoid her eyes. "I had a lot of time to think in the hospital, and I'm not so sure that we're compatible." I glanced at her face. It contorted in an obvious state of confusion. "And I don't think we were behaving quite properly. It was too much temptation for me."

I glanced at her again. Her lips pointed and her face narrowed into a piercing grimace.

"Temptation? Is that what you think I am—some sort of temptress? It's because of what I just said about virgins, isn't it?"

"No," I said, though that wasn't entirely true.

"Do you want to know what I think about you?"

"Probably not."

"I think you're a self-righteous prude who thinks too highly of himself."

"Well, I'm glad we got that out in the open." Her words stung me because I sensed they were true.

Phillip yelled for Shenan again. "Give me a minute!" she yelled, then turned to me. "Well, I hope you get your boat, Jim, but it sounds like you're going to have to find someone less tempting, someone a little purer, to work with you."

Feeling wounded and angry at the way she dismissed Phillip, I found myself saying things to spite her. "Perhaps you wouldn't make a good puller anyway."

"What do you mean?"

"I'm just saying that I'm not going to hire you to do a man's job when you're barely willing to do the woman's job you already have."

Her hand seemed to come out of nowhere as it slapped me hard across the face. She scowled at me with her fists balled up on her hips. Apparently, I didn't show enough pain, for she leaned toward me and shoved me forcefully. My boots caught against the gunnel. I tripped backward, flailing my arms to regain balance. It didn't work. I felt myself falling, then splashing, into the freezing water. My muscles tightened as the frigid water stabbed my skin at every point. Water filled my boots, which I kicked away. I concentrated hard on holding my breath and forced my arms to return me to the surface. By the time I reached it and opened my eyes, Shenan was already on the *Nereid* bumping Phillip's shoulder as she went by. I swam to the boat and grabbed the gunnel and hung on desperately while I caught my breath. My first thought was that my boots were gone forever.

Joe came over and helped me aboard with his good arm. "Are you okay?" he asked. I stumbled aboard, dripping-wet, and collapsed onto the deck. Leaning against the gunnel, I bent my knees together and pulled my elbows against my sides to conserve heat.

"I'm fine," I said. My teeth chattered between every few words. "I'm going to need . . . new boots."

Joe furrowed his brow. "What happened? I thought you got along real well."

"We did . . . until . . . until I messed everything up." I clamped my jaw tight, worried the chattering would break a tooth.

"Are you guys gonna make up?"

"I don't . . . know."

"Go inside. Once you're warm, we'll go to the *Nereid* for dinner."

"I'll eat here." I wanted to explain that I couldn't eat food prepared by Shenan that night but talking was too laborious.

"No, I want you to eat with us. We have important things to talk about."

\*\*\*

I changed into dry clothes—the least dirty ones I had. I tried covering the fish smell with the cheap cologne Joe bought me. I took a whiff of my shirt, which still smelled horrible. It didn't matter—trying to smell good for Shenan was pointless now.

It was getting late, and the weak sun had faded more by the time I climbed aboard the *Nereid*.

"Here comes the swimmer," Phillip said, laughing and slapping me on the back. "Are you okay?"

"Yes."

Shenan delivered plates of salmon and did an excellent job ignoring me. Making eye contact with no one, she clamped her jaw tight. I didn't even try speaking to her. Watching her pass out plates to the likes of Steve and Phillip made me feel sorry for her and made me even more regretful for the things I had said.

I reached to take my paper plate from her, but she plopped it on the fish hold instead. Phillip raised his eyebrows and Steve let out a small chuckle. I took the plate and started to eat. At least Shenan had learned a great deal about preparing salmon. It was tasty, but I didn't feel hungry.

Joe looked at Phillip like they had some implicit understanding. Phillip said, "Shenan, can you join us for a second?"

"I'm not eating."

"Okay, but we need to talk to you."

"If it's about Jim, there's nothing to talk about."

Phillip looked at me again like he was going to laugh. All of this was somehow quite amusing to him. "No, it's not about Jim, and we *do* need to talk."

Shenan came on deck, plopping herself down on one of the holds with her arms crossed. Phillip looked at Joe skeptically, then turned to Shenan again. "There's something Joe and I want to talk to you about." Steve nearly laughed now.

"Yes?" she said, thrusting her jaw forward.

"As you know, Joe can't really fish because of his arm and Jim can't do it by himself." The salmon grew tasteless in my mouth, and a feeling of dread poured into my stomach. "Joe asked if I thought you could help him on his boat. I told him you hadn't worked at fishing, but that you're eager to. He just needs a second set of hands to pull the net and pick the fish."

Shenan's face changed incrementally. From a stubborn refusal to listen, it transfigured into a highbrowed, snooty expression. Phillip continued. "Of course, this is entirely up to you, and you're in no way obligated to—"

"I'll do it," she said.

"If you don't want . . ." He looked up in surprise. "Oh, you'll do it? Don't you want to hear more?"

"I just want to make sure that Joe wants me as a puller and not as a cook or a maid?"

"I can't fish," Joe said, "but I can still cook. You'll take turns cooking with me and Jim. But I mostly need you to help Jim. Even though we're halfway through the season, I'll pay you ten percent of the season earnings."

"When do you want me to start?" Shenan asked.

"Tomorrow. I'll clear off the bench by me and Jim's bunks. If you want to, you can get your things and come over tonight."

I glanced at Shenan to see what she was thinking. To my surprise, her eyes no longer avoided mine. She looked me directly with one eyebrow cocked high.

She turned to Joe and used her southern decorum voice. "Thank you, Joe. It's about time someone realized I can do more than a woman's job. And I would be glad to help you and your deck hand, if he is in so much need of help. I'll go pack my things now." She stood and went to the cabin.

I looked up at the twilight sky and exhaled slowly. Oh Lord, I thought, the three of us were going to sleep in the bow of that little boat? Joe told Shenan we needed help after everything I'd just said? I placed my plate down, feeling apprehensive about the situation. All my recent thoughts about avoiding Shenan seemed laughable now, for the Cherokee Mermaid would now be within an arm's reach of me twenty-four hours a day.

## Chapter 7

# The Ghost of the *Mikilak*

Things have taken a turn for the worse here in Pedro Bay. A man is dead. He was a dentist from the Lower Forty-Eight who came to Alaska for a world-class fishing trip, but the trip ended in tragedy. His body was found on a riverbank not far from here. Bite marks and shredded flesh left no secret that he had been killed by a wild animal and I am the closest wildlife agent for a hundred miles.

It's been two days since Finn Nickolai brought me the news. As the region's Wildlife Trooper, it was my duty to investigate. I'm nearly certain the man was killed by a bear—most likely a brown bear—but I'm waiting for proof. Today, I flew his mangled, partially decomposed body to Anchorage where the state medical examiner will determine the official cause of his fate. If the results say bear—and they will—I will have to identify the culprit and ensure it is no longer a threat to people. Most likely, I will have to euthanize it.

But finding the right bear is not going to be easy. The bears are everywhere this summer. There are many bears because there were many salmon, but the salmon are mostly gone, and the berries have not yet ripened. This is the time when the old bears grow hungry, and the villagers of Pedro Bay are growing anxious. The situation reminds me that my job is not only to protect people from bears, but to protect bears from people.

The path that led me to Wildlife Trooper is somewhat convoluted. For many years—perhaps the best years of my life—I worked in the field as a research biologist. The bulk of my writings center around this period and the harrowing adventures and unusual people I met in the Alaskan bush. But as an expert on wolves, my expertise was increasingly sought out by the public, the press, local governments, and even by the senate in Juneau. They promoted me to a Region Supervisor. It was important work, but it was no longer fun. The only thing I flew during this period was a desk.

At the age of forty-five, I quit. It was then that I worked an odd assortment of jobs as a bush pilot, a fishing guide, and a small-scale farmer. But I missed the field and I missed the animals, so I turned my back on that chapter and returned to the Department of Fish and Game. They made me the Deputy Director of the Division of Wildlife Conservation. A few years later, I served as Director during the worldwide imbroglio over aerial wolf hunts. Those years took their toll on me. I lost weight and felt increasingly tired. I received hints that the Governor considered me for the position of Commissioner of the Alaska Department of Fish and Game. I was one step away from running the whole shebang. But I was through with politics and administration, and I yearned to be back in the wilderness. I retired to the shores of Lake Iliamna, took up work as bush pilot again, got involved in more conservation issues, and started to write about my life.

But I needed a reason to get out of the cabin—especially during the cold, dark months. When a position opened for an Alaska Wildlife Trooper, I decided to apply. I inquired about the age limit and found that there was none (which was probably an oversight), so I went to the Trooper Academy and passed the physical training. I aced the shooting requirements. I believe that to this day, I am the oldest graduate ever from the Trooper Academy. Some people said I was going through a late-life crisis, taking a huge pay cut from the career I once had, but I knew what I was doing. I have been happy flying in the field again, working with hunters, trappers, and fishermen—and, of course, the animals.

That is, I was happy until now. During the heated meeting with the villagers tonight, I felt that this situation could explode just like the aerial wolf hunt drama. The general attitude of the village also reminded me of the events that occurred in Newhalen in 1995, and that situation could have gotten much worse. Newhalen is a town not far from here on Lake Iliamna. In '95, the bears were more numerous than usual. There were run-ins between men and bears as they fished elbow-to-elbow in the rivers. Then a bear mauled a German tourist. Within days, five brown bears, including a sow and two cubs, were found dead, shot by unknown persons. Apparently, someone (or some group) had engaged the bears in a small war of retaliation. People across Alaska deplored the bear killings, demanding the perpetrators be found and punished. The president of the tribal council retorted that urban animal rights groups were out of touch and were trying to impose their values on traditional cultures. It was a mess. Eventually, after months of investigation, authorities found the perpetrators and arrested them.

That situation could repeat itself here in Pedro Bay, and that is what I hope to avoid. I must balance the needs of the wildlife with the safety of the public. I must act before the villagers do. If I don't, this could escalate into another bear war.

I outlined the state's plan to the villagers tonight. It would take time, I cautioned. We have no idea which bear killed the dentist, but animal DNA samples were taken from the body. All we must do, I explained, is tranquilize suspect bears in the region, take saliva and hair samples, radio collar them, and send the samples to Anchorage for DNA matching. Once a match was found, we would track the bear and determine the appropriate course of action— aversive conditioning, relocation, or euthanization.

The difficult part is getting the samples. I explained that a helicopter with tranquilizing equipment would be dispatched from Anchorage and would arrive in a few days, weather permitting. In the meantime, we had to be patient. Some of the villagers protested that the plan was far too complicated. They said that they could have killed the bear by now. Meanwhile, they added, the state left them vulnerable to a man-killing beast.

Then the wolf came up. A man reported that a black wolf had been seen on the outskirts of the village over the past few months. It looked dangerous, he said. He theorized that the wolf, not a bear, mauled the dentist. I did my best to nip this theory in the bud. I said that I knew this wolf. She was an outcast from her pack and had been roaming the north shore of the lake the past few seasons, probably on her way to find a new pack. This, I said, is a common occurrence for young wolves. Though she approached humans a few times, she was not dangerous. Wolves—especially wolves on their own—virtually never attack people. Besides, I said, it was a non-issue. Brown bear hair and brown bear DNA was found all over the dentist. The man replied that this did not negate the fact that a hungry wolf could be dangerous. He added that if a child in the village were killed by the wolf, their blood would be on my hands. Comments like this lead me to believe that this town is a simmering coal in a hay field. A few rash decisions could turn the situation into more than a bear war—it might involve wolves as well. It would be man versus beast, and it would be on the front page of every paper in the state.

Returning to the cabin tonight, I felt drained by my interactions with humans. Thankfully, 1969 is still here to distract me.

*\*\*\**

Back on the *Mikilak*, I told Joe I would clear off the bench in our small berthing space to make room for Shenan. I was still a little shocked by the decision to bring Shenan to our boat but said nothing to Joe about it. In truth, it was an obvious solution. As boat owner, he made a logical decision to benefit himself and his crew. The only thing to do was to remove the remaining canned food from the storage bench to clear a space for Shenan to sleep.

The berthing cabin in the bow of the *Mikilak* lay a few steps below the pilot house. The pilot house contained the controls for the boat, a tiny table, storage cabinets, and a cook stove. Like most boats back then, there was no bathroom—we merely had a bucket and the water around us and the occasional excursion ashore to relieve ourselves.

The *Mikilak* had only one set of bunk beds, which ran along the starboard side. I slept on top. A vaulted portion of the overhead contained four small portholes to let in light. The port side of this triangle-shaped room had a bench with storage space inside. There was another smaller cabinet above it with cupboard doors. As we had depleted many of our foodstuffs, we had more room for Shenan's personal belongings. I didn't want Shenan to have to sleep on the bench as it seemed the indentations from the hatch covers would be uncomfortable. Even though the hard plywood bunk I slept on was not much better, I decided to give it to her. It was the least I could do after the way I spoke to her.

When I finished moving my sleeping bag down to the cabinet, she appeared at the top of the steps with a backpack and a sleeping bag. I pointed out the space I'd made for her on my bunk. "You can sleep up there."

"You don't need to give me your rack."

"I thought you'd be more comfortable—"

"Joe offered the bench, and that's fine. Besides, it's shorter—you wouldn't fit over there. Now if you would please let me get settled."

As I squeezed by the rolled sleeping bag in her arms, she turned away.

"Look, Shenan—"

"We don't need to talk," she replied, cutting me off.

"Yes, we do. We're going to be working together now."

"But we don't need to talk about us."

It was no use. I climbed the two steps on my way out and found Joe in the stern where we often sat and talked at night. We sprawled out on the fish holds and watched as Shenan made one more trip to the *Nereid* and returned with a guitar case and two more bags. I looked at Joe and wondered where we would put everything.

Shenan placed her guitar upright in the main cabin and came back to the doorway. "If you gentlemen don't mind going down to the berthing compartment for a moment, I would like to use the bucket."

Joe explained where the bar of soap was before we climbed down to the cabin to wait. To make conversation, he discussed the fishing prospects of the Nushagak basin versus the Ugashik. In a few minutes, Shenan reappeared in the main cabin to tell us we could return to the stern. "Joe," she said, "I'm going to clean up downstairs for a while if you don't mind." He nodded his head and we traded places again. All this switching was going to be burdensome, I thought.

Laying outside again, I told Joe about the boat for sale. He said I would make a fine boat captain but said

I should finish college first. I said I could fish in the summers. "Perhaps," he said. We lapsed into one of our prolonged silences and languished in the unusually warm night.

I don't know why we stayed up so late that night. Maybe we weren't comfortable with the new sleeping situation, or maybe it was the tolerably warm night, or both. I was comfortable in jeans and a long-sleeve shirt but needed no jacket.

"It must be in the mid-sixties," I said to Joe.

"Maybe."

After midnight, it got almost dark—dark enough to see the brighter stars. The navigation lights of forty fishing boats rocked gently around us like red, white and green fireflies hovering over a pond. The air was still. The warm glow of lantern-light beamed through the windows of twenty cabins. The gentle din of other conversations drifted across the water as well as the laughs of men passing their free time on this unusually temperate night. I laid out on one of the fish holds, contemplating the strange night and the almost surreal presence of Shenan. I imagined it was strange for Joe, too, but had no way of knowing.

After nearly an hour, the tranquility was disturbed by the sound of the door latch. I imagined Shenan had gone to sleep, but she appeared in the door in a long white nightgown. I supposed she brought that to Alaska because she was sleeping around men and it covered her figure more than anything. She came out of the cabin and held her outstretched hand over the side of the boat, apparently testing the temperature. She never looked at me. She went briefly into the cabin and returned with the guitar. Almost trance-like, she walked the narrow deck beside the cabin toward the bow. Like a tight-rope performer, she placed one foot in front of the other, her arms outstretched, her right hand against the windows of the cabin, her left hand holding the neck of the guitar high above the water. She disappeared around the pilot house.

I sat up, leaning my back against the gunnel, waiting for the music. In a minute, I heard the first plaintive notes of a guitar being tuned, one string against the next until they synchronized, then a chord, then a voice humming to find the key, then more chords, some of them in a minor key, enchanting, somewhat disconcerting. Shenan was an adroit guitar-player, not only strumming all the chords in their various iterations but adding licks and notes between.

She coughed several times as if to clear her throat, then started to sing.

*"I'm just a poor wayfaring stranger,*
*A-travelin' through this world of woe.*
*But there's no sickness, toil, nor danger,*
*In that bright world to which I go..."*

It was a song I had not heard for some time—a melancholy spiritual from the past. I liked it, but it also discomforted me with its minor keys and predictions of worldly trouble. Her singing voice was sweet, almost child-like, not what I had pictured from someone with a biting tongue and the power to shove a man overboard. She had trouble hitting the low notes, but the mid-tones resonated clear and bright out across the water. As she continued to sing, the faint din from the other boats subsided. Black silhouettes appeared on decks looking for the music's source. They must have been close enough to barely see her—a faint woman in a white gown on the bow of the *Mikilak*. In the next lines, her voice rose with the melody, the words of each line trailing off into the night.

*"I'm going there to see my father,*

*I'm going there no more to roam.*
*I'm just a-goin' over Jordan.*
*I'm just a-goin' over home."*

I looked at Joe. His eyes were alert and probing, almost tearful. He was an old man, and it was a sad song of death. Perhaps it made him think of something or someone. I wanted to go to the bow. I wanted to take her and hold her as I had done only two days before. I wanted to do that and more, but we had argued. We argued over our relationship, and we argued about sin. Away from her, I promised God that I would leave her alone, but my promises faded in her presence. Who was she? What was she doing singing in a nightgown in the middle of nowhere? Perhaps she was a temptress. Perhaps she was an angel. I was half-asleep listening to the musical net she cast in my direction.

*"I know dark clouds will gather 'round me,*
*I know my way is rough and steep,*
*But beauteous fields lie just beyond me,*
*Where souls redeemed their vigil keep."*

It was on this night that Shenan became a legend. Some fishermen had seen her briefly that summer, but most had not. It was only then that most of the men on Bristol Bay were made aware of her presence. Standing on the decks of their boats, they searched for her across the water. For weeks, they had been cut off from women, cut off from beauty, cut off from music, and suddenly, a woman's voice came like a ghost in the darkness. Several years later, while eating lunch in the Sea Tavern, I heard one old salt talk about the night he saw a white ghost singing on the bow of a small boat. But then, he said, it might have been a sea-nymph warning the fisherman of the future. She had a beautiful, flowing white gown, he said, and a guitar, and sang that she was a stranger roaming through the world. "I saw it with my own eyes," he said, "Don't let anyone tell you there ain't spirits out there." I chuckled to myself, not wanting to spoil the man's mystical experience. I didn't tell him that I knew who she was—that I knew her very well and had touched her and kissed her. Besides, I couldn't exactly say that he was wrong. She was a ghost, and a temptress, and a spirit. She was indeed a strange thing roaming through this world.

At the conclusion of the song, she appeared again and delicately walked the narrow freeboard the same way she had left. She looked at me briefly this time, her eyes dark and resolute, then looked at Joe.

"Good night, Joe," she said.

"Good night, Shenandoah."

She returned to the cabin.

I looked at Joe. "I guess we're not even on speaking terms."

"It seems so."

"Sorry I made this so difficult." He didn't say anything. "To be honest," I added, "I don't even know why she's so mad."

We both lay on the fish holds watching the sky above us. Finally, he said, "You are a very nice man, Jim, but sometimes you talk like a white man."

Turning his words over in my mind, I peered at the stars moving in the sky. "What does that mean?" I asked.

I waited for an answer, but none ever came. After some minutes of frustration, I said, "Well, I may talk like a white man, but at least I talk."

I heard the faintest chuckle from him. "We should go to bed now," he said.

I followed him into the pilot house where he rapped gently on the berthing door.

"Come in," said the voice inside. I opened the hatch and found her bundled in her sleeping bag, her eyes closed. Joe and I climbed into our bunks and undressed there, kicking our clothes into piles beyond the reach of our feet. A breeze blew in through the portholes, and I lay awake for a long time pondering the way that I talked.

## Chapter 8

# The Littlest One

In the morning, the sun beamed through one of the portholes. Shenan was somewhere outside, coughing up a storm. In a brain fog, the events of the previous evening crowded into my mind—the argument, the shove overboard, Shenan bringing her things, and her song in the night—and I wondered if my memory played tricks on me. I leaned over the edge of my bunk and saw a folded sleeping bag and a pair of small rubber boots and knew that at least most of it had been real. I threw on jeans and a flannel shirt and went up where I found Joe scooping eggs at the table.

"Geez, is she okay?" I asked, pointing toward the stern.

"She said her asthma makes her cough every morning."

I thought I should check on her, so leaned my head out the hatch. "Are you okay?"

"I'm fine," she said, doubled up on the aft fish hold with her head over the side.

"Are you seasick?"

"No."

"Do you need anything?"

"Just let me be for a minute."

Reluctantly, I left her alone and went to the table. In the pilot house, there was an odd-shaped table with a built-in bench on one side and a single stool on the other. I sat in the single spot in the front and began eating. Shenan came into the pilot house a few minutes later, apparently recovered, and said nothing. She wore her olive-green slickers, which looked new.

"Are you feeling better?"

"It was just my asthma." She turned to Joe. "That smells wonderful, Joe. Thank you so much for breakfast."

We ate for several minutes in silence, then Joe said, "We'd better head out." He started the engine from the pilot's seat, then went on deck to untie us from the *Nereid*. I got up to help.

"I got it," Shenan said, motioning for me to stay in my seat.

After the two shoved off from the *Nereid*, Joe returned to the helm while Shenan sat outside. We pulled away from Shenan's former boat and picked up speed. She sat near the edge watching the ocean glide past us with her hair blowing in the wind. I couldn't judge her mood by the expression on her face. It was emotionless except for a possible hint of sadness. I wished I could cheer her.

I did the dishes as we cruised to our chosen fishing spot. While most of the boats darted around looking for fish, Joe was much more patient. He picked a spot and stuck to it. I made some coffee, handed Joe a mug, and poured two more. Carrying the coffee outside, I noticed it was chillier than the night before when Shenan sang to all the boats. The day, like most days, was a cloudy one.

I extended the cup of coffee.

"No, thanks." She hugged her legs to her chest and maintained her forward gaze.

"C'mon, Shenan. We can't do this—especially now."

"Do what?"

"You know what I mean. We have to work together."

"I just don't need coffee. It would probably give me another coughing fit."

"Okay, I'll dump it back in the pot and you can have it later if you want."

"Would you like me to tend the coffee pot and keep it warm and fill your cup when it gets cold?" she asked.

"Don't be ridiculous." I went back to the pilot house. I had planned to tell her how much I enjoyed her singing, but there was a fat chance of that now.

I went to the berthing space to get my boots and rain jacket. Having lost my rubber boots, I had to wear plain leather ones instead. Bending over I saw Shenan's small rubber boots. I liked having them there with me. They made the whole boat feel like a home. I realized my clothes smelled horribly, so I grabbed the bottle of cologne and dabbed some on. I had just put it away when Shenan came in.

She'd come for the boots. Bent over, I saw her sniff the air. It was awkward trying to get around each other. Her elbow touched my knee. She jerked it to her side. I joined Joe in the pilot house thinking he might be better company. It's not that I expected him to talk, but at least it would be a friendly silence. Shenan came up wearing her boots and poured the coffee into her cup.

"It's a shame about your boots, Jim," she said.

For the life of me, I couldn't tell if she was being remorseful or spiteful. "I'll get by."

Cradling the mug in her hands, she went to stand by Joe. I saw her eye the cranberry float hanging in the corner near him. "It looks pretty there," she said. We stood in silence for some time watching the horizon as we crossed the bay. In the distance, a humpback whale breached. It excited Shenan immensely. Joe did his best to answer her questions about humpback whales, telling her that they had returned from a winter in Hawaii. Joe's mood seemed almost jovial. It was obvious that he enjoyed Shenan's company.

"Joe, can I ask you a question?"

"Sure."

"Why didn't you name the *Mikilak* after a girl? It seems like all the other boats are named after women."

"I did."

Shenan lowered the mug from her lips and turned to him. "Really? Is Mikilak a name?"

"It means *littlest one*. That's what her father called her."

"Whose father?"

"A girl I knew."

"And where is she now?"

"She's married."

"Oh, I see." She waited to see if he would say more. He didn't. "Well, I'll tell you one thing, Joe." Shenan stepped closer to him and hugged him from the side as he sat at the wheel. "She missed a good one." He smiled.

Minutes later, Joe asked us to pray. "There's enough of us now to do this right." He let go of the wheel, which generally stayed on a forward heading, and reached for our hands. She hesitated to take mine.

"You don't have to do this if you don't want to," I said.

"No, I'd be happy to." She loosely took my hand. It was clear that her good spirits had not changed her mind about me. As soon as Joe said, "Amen," she let go.

"You two check the net."

As we stepped outside, I tied the door open so we could yell back and forth with Joe. In the stern, I showed Shenan how to inspect the net. "This is the most important thing of all," I said, touching a cleat where the corkline was securely knotted, "making sure the whole net is tied to the boat. "This," I said, indicating a loop at the end of the corkline, "is the end. We'll hook the buoy to it.

Now, you can work backwards from here and make sure all three shackles are connected."

"What's a shackle?"

"A shackle is a section of net fifty fathoms long. Three shackles is the maximum length allowed by law."

Shenan searched through the intricate mess, inspecting the corkline one arm's length at a time.

"I thought you guys didn't hold hands when you prayed," she said.

"We don't. That's what he meant when he said we could pray the right way—because there's three of us."

"I hope God doesn't mind that there's a pile of Playboys under the bench."

"Those aren't mine."

"Oh, and I'm sure you've never looked at them." I paused too long. "Don't worry, Jim. I'm not being judgmental," she said, running the corkline through her hands. "I'm not always sleeping when I'm sleeping in."

My thoughts strayed so far that I almost startled when Joe yelled, "Okay, get ready."

I handed her the buoy. "I see. Is that because you're surrounded by so many men?"

Her face contorted into a look that was equal parts disgust and amusement. "Ha! Not hardly." She clipped the buoy to the corkline. "Everyone has tension that needs to be released."

"Of course," I said, trying to cover the fact that I didn't know a damn thing about women.

"All right," Joe said, "Let her roll."

Shenan hesitated. I cocked my head toward the sea. She swung the orange buoy over the stern. It rose high in the air before splashing into the water. Together, we fed the net over the roller. The boat moved slowly forward. Once enough net was in the water, it started to pull itself out. We watched it to prevent knots and snags until all three shackles went over the roller. Then, we watched and waited. Joe came and stood in the doorway. Shenan and I leaned on opposite gunnels. It started to drizzle.

"Now what do we do?"

"Just wait."

"I noticed you're wearing cologne."

"Oh, yeah, I thought it might make it easier to deal with the smell."

"My dad says you shouldn't get human smells on your bait. I hope your cologne doesn't keep the fish away."

"We're not bass fishing in Virginia."

She threw her hood up as the rain picked up, hastily crossed her arms and turned away from the wind.

"Let's not argue and just focus on working," I said.

"Who's arguing?"

I felt my jaw clench. We stood silent for fifteen minutes as we drifted in the water and watched the corkline. The rain pattered on the gray water around us. She refused to look in my direction, but I could not help stealing glances at her—small tendrils of curly, black hair escaped out the front of her hood—and my mind raced with thoughts of what she did when she was sleeping in.

Finally, when the rain turned into a downpour, the net showed life. We watched the water with more enthusiasm now. I was glad to have something to distract my thoughts. It wasn't a huge score, but the hits came slow and steady.

After an hour, the activity died down, but the rain held up. "Let's haul her in," Joe said. Shenan and I lifted the covers from the aft fish hold. I grabbed the line and began to haul. Shenan came to my side and pulled. Side-by-side we pulled until the first sockeye salmon appeared over the roller.

"Do you have your pick?" I asked.

She showed me the small tool, a handle with a curved piece of wire on one end and a flat razor on the other. "Yes, but I don't know how to use it."

"I'll show you. Get that one," I said, pointing to the first fish.

Shenan grabbed it, but it was caught tight in the webbing. I grabbed the second one and yanked it out. The third was barely hanging, so I grabbed the net and jerked it, slamming the fish into the fish hold. I pulled more net and picked the fourth salmon with the tool in my hand. Shenan still struggled with the first fish.

"Like this," I said, reaching for her hand. I placed my hand over hers and squeezed her fingers into the fish's gills. She looked over my arm, watching to see what I did. With my hand over hers, I used the hook to pull the tight webbing over the thickest part of the fish's body, alternating between the spine and the belly until the fish was free in our hands. She stood there for a moment smiling at the wriggling fish in her hand, then tossed it into the hold. "Now get more net," I said. "If we wait too long, it will back into the prop."

She grabbed the net and pulled. "There, try that one," I said. "It's just the same." After a few yanks back and forth, she pulled it out and threw it into the hold. Standing there, dripping in the rain, more hair escaping from her hood, she smiled. She caught me looking at her. She put on a dour expression as if she were not at all impressed by herself and went furiously back to work. Within minutes we worked smoothly together. "Okay, you see that one," I said. "That's a hanger. The webbing is already past the thickest part of the body. Just grab the net and fling him out." She slammed him to the deck.

We pulled and picked the whole net. At one point, I told Shenan to pick up the fish around our feet and throw them into the holds. She did it without reservation. I probably picked three-quarters of the fish, but Shenan had certainly done more than Joe could have.

"Very good," Joe said. "Let's go again."

Shenan beat me to the buoy and threw it over the side. Joe kicked the transmission into forward gear and the net snaked out over the roller. We waited until another school hit us.

"Haul her in."

Shenan and I attacked the net this time. She placed her boot on the transom, pulling hard. She fought to be the first one to the fish. She wasn't—I made sure of that. Still, she improved with every fish. I occasionally helped with the tricky ones—the ones that had to come out backwards, or that required net cutting—but by the end of the day, she was a competent puller.

The crane on the receiving ship, the tender, lowered its brailer down to us. We filled it as quickly as possible. We used the peughsticks—long poles with hooks on the end—to grab the salmon and slide or throw them into the large bag. As we watched the crane lift the brailer from the *Mikilak*, I wondered what ran through Shenan's mind. Fish scales covered her cheeks, face, and raincoat. They were in her hair and on her neck. She was covered in slime, and rain dripped from the tip of her nose. I remember her often this way—covered in shimmering scales. She looked small and vulnerable, but she could work very hard. She probably didn't know that I gazed at her. Her attention was on the brailer rising to the tender. Her face beamed as she stood in the slimy, bloody waters of the deck. I could see that she was proud of that brailer, and rightly so, for Shenan proved that she could be a fisherman.

# Chapter 9

# Temptation

I went to bed that night to the sound of raindrops pattering on the wooden hull over my head. I awoke the next morning to entirely different weather. The sunlight beamed into the portholes as I leaned over to see Shenan. She lay sleeping. She was a mess, her hair in tangles, her skin covered in fish scales. She lay on her side with her head resting on her arm instead of her pillow.

After some time, Shenan shuffled on the bench. Apparently dissatisfied with the outcome, she punched her pillow and rolled onto her back. Even with her eyes closed, she looked uncomfortable. It seemed she had not slept well. Perhaps it was because the sleeping bag was the only mattress she had on the hard, wooden bench. Joe and I didn't have mattresses either, but our plywood bunks were not indented by hatches. Shenan rolled over, adjusting her body as best she could. I would offer to trade places again but doubted she would accept.

Minutes later, I put my clothes on while still in my rack. Once dressed, I swung quietly to the deck and snuck out to make breakfast. There weren't many choices, so I cooked up some eggs with cheese. Joe joined me in the pilot house. We talked while Shenan slept. Over breakfast, Joe and I determined to head to the same spot as the day before. Even though we hadn't caught a lot of fish, it was better than nothing.

We cruised for half an hour before Joe asked me to wake Shenan.

I sat on Joe's bunk, elbows on my knees. "Shenan," I said. I placed my hand on her shoulder, shaking it gently. "Shenan, it's time to wake up." She opened her eyes and looked at me. She was tired, with bags under bloodshot eyes. I wanted to keep my hand on her shoulder but removed it as soon as she woke.

"Okay," she said. "I'll be right up."

"Do you want a cup of coffee?"

"Yes."

"I'll bring you one."

"No. I'll be up in a second."

"Okay. There's a fresh pot on the stove."

I went up the two small steps, through the cabin and joined Joe on the deck. We listened to the fishing report on the marine radio as Shenan went through her morning coughing fit in the berthing compartment. The droning voice announced that Fish & Game would close the fishing period at noon. Thus far, the salmon numbers were quite low, and the government needed more salmon to make it into the rivers where they would breed and ensure future generations of salmon. This was going to be an unbelievably short fishing period. The weather had changed dramatically since the day before—there was no breeze and sunlight beamed onto our little boat. Shenan came on deck with a cup of coffee in her hands.

"This spot is good," Joe called out. I nodded and cast the buoy over the stern-roller. Shenan set her coffee down to help me guide the net as it rolled over the stern of the boat. In less than a minute, we ran out all three shackles. Shenan picked up her mug again and closed her hands around it like she was trying to warm them.

"They're closing the fishing today at noon," I said.

"Oh, really?"

"Yeah."

"I guess we'll have to do the best we can." Finishing her coffee, she returned the mug to the cabin, then rejoined me in the stern, unbuttoning the top few buttons of her raincoat. "We didn't pray," she said.

"Joe did that before you came out."

She reached back and rubbed the muscles between her shoulder blades.

"You sore?"

"Not really."

I didn't believe her, of course. She had done more work the day before than she had done the whole summer—perhaps in her whole life. She rolled her head, trying to work the kinks out of her neck. I wanted to give her a massage and wondered if it would be appropriate to offer one.

"It's okay to say you're sore, Shenan. I would expect it."

"What do you care anyway?"

"I don't really care. Even I'm a little sore."

"What do you want me to say? Yes, I'm sore and weak and I can't do this job. Would that make you feel better?"

"Not at all."

Joe yelled from the pilothouse, "You guys see anything?"

"Not yet," I shouted back.

Any remaining clouds had burned off now. The sun beat down on our dark rubber raincoats, so I decided to remove mine. I was already hot and hadn't even started working.

"Shenan, you've got the wrong idea."

"Really? Tell me where I'm wrong. You think that I'm not cut out to do a man's job. You think that I'm a Buddhist who would bring bad luck to your boat. You think that I'm a sinful influence—a seductress. You only like virgin boats and virgin girls. And, you want me to stay away from you because I'm too much temptation. Is that not right?"

"I didn't say you'd bring bad luck to my boat."

"Is that the only thing I got wrong?"

Ensnared by my own words, I tried to tease apart what she got right and what she got wrong. That was the most troubling thing of all—though I hadn't said all those words, she had accurately described some of my thoughts, and if that is what I thought, then perhaps I truly was a self-righteous jerk.

"You see," she said after I didn't respond, "I think I have the right idea."

I turned my attention to the net and wallowed in self-loathing. We watched and waited. As we waited, small pods of fish hit the net—three here, five there—nothing spectacular, then the action died down.

"I think they're gone," she said.

I grunted.

"You seem down."

"Maybe."

We were silent again. After some time, she backed away from the roller. Out of the corner of my eye I saw her remove her raincoat. "I think this is the warmest day yet," she said, placing her coat near the cabin.

"Decided to be like me, huh?"

"I thought I might get some sun today."

"We'll probably get cold again when we're wet."

"I know. I've been on a fishing boat for three weeks."

She came and leaned on the roller next to me with only a tank-top under her overall straps. The coffee, or the outdoor activity, had dispelled most of the fatigue from her face. Her hair was done up in a tight bun high on her head. Dried fish scales sequined her hair and cheeks.

Her elbow rested a few inches from mine on the roller as we looked out over the lifeless net. "Let me know if I'm being too much temptation."

"About that . . . About the things I said the other night. I'm sorry. I didn't mean to suggest you were a bad person because you're not. Not even close. Just don't pay attention to half the things I say."

"Did you say something?"

"Ha. Ha."

"Don't worry, I'll get over it."

"And the part about not hiring you to do a man's job came out all wrong. I was only saying that because I felt like we hadn't kept the deal with Phillip."

"I know that." She paused, then added, "And I'm sorry for what I said. I obviously don't think you're a bad person either. You can be self-righteous, but when you keep that in check, you're a pretty swell guy."

"Gee, thanks."

"Just make sure you keep it in check."

"I'll do my best. And one more thing—the temptation thing—I wasn't suggesting that you do anything on purpose."

"Good," she said. She looked at me, bit her lower lip, and played with the strap of her bib overalls. "Because I'd never do anything like that on purpose."

"Stop it." I laughed, but I meant it. The playful gesture distracted me to no end. "Maybe we should talk about salmon or something."

She let go of the overall strap, which snapped against her tank top. "Okay," she said, then turned her attention to the long line of floating corks behind us.

We talked about the life cycle of salmon and what a strange system mother nature had devised in creating a long, grueling journey to test which salmon would get to mate. A big splash interrupted our musings. A barrage of fish struck the net.

Shenan stood up straight. I looked at Joe. If he wasn't such a silent man, I think he might have whooped and hollered. But then again, maybe he wouldn't—he never seemed to care too much about fish or money.

We watched for signs of salmon in the net. They hit high and low. Water spewed into the air from several sections of the net. Salmon hit the top so fast they looped over the corkline, caught in web cocoons. Other floats jerked and bobbed with frenetic energy. The hits kept coming. Shenan stared, her eyes wide with wonder. The net throbbed and moved like a live animal.

"Are they all around us?" she asked, turning her head as if trying to see them.

"Probably. Picture thousands of silver bullets that we can't see, shooting under our feet, shooting behind us, shooting beyond our net. I bet that for every one we've got, there's a hundred more escaping around us." I looked completely around. There was not another boat in sight. "There might be a hundred-thousand just in this area."

She looked at me and smiled, the first unadulterated smile I'd seen in days. The energy of the salmon possessed her. "This is amazing, Jim," she said. "This is how people are supposed to make a living."

"They can keep their factories and their corporate offices," I said, "we're doing it the real way."

She smiled—not just smiled—but smiled at me specifically. I knew then that I would do anything to keep her doing that.

"Alright, you two," Joe said in his slow, punctuated speech. "Best get that thing out of the water."

Shenan and I came together and pulled. The net rose from the water full of jerking, throbbing fish. It was heavy. The first salmon over the roller appeared on my side. I let go of the net to pull it. Shenan's wiry but strong arms kept the net from regressing over the roller.

"Keep pulling," I said.

"Okay, as long as you can keep up," she said, pulling harder.

The fish appeared in large clumps, some in tangled messes. Perhaps we had left the net in too long, I wondered. Joe left the transmission in neutral and came back to help. He held the net with his good arm while Shenan and I picked the fish. The floorboards thumped from fish hitting the deck. The fish fell equally fast on Shenan's side. I moved faster. I got a tangled one and struggled with it—untwisting the net, trying to decide which side of the net it should come from. One thump, two thumps. Shenan's fish slammed the deck.

"You need help, Jim?" she asked. Finally, I threw the little fish into the hold.

"No, I'm good." I looked at her. A sheen of sweat and sea spray covered her face, neck and chest. It soaked the little white tank top that peeked over her bib. Drops trickled between her breasts. She saw me looking. "Concentrate, Jim."

I tugged on the net, lifting a huge cluster of frantic fish out of the water. The work grew mechanical. Twist, grab the head, pick the web, throw, next one, grab the net, slam to the deck, pull, next one, cut one strand, drop the fish, next one…

I found rhythm. Shenan fell behind. I reached for a fish on her side. One cut and the fish dropped. Now my side—a puller, extract, toss to the hold, pull more net. I tried to catch my breath. I glanced at Shenan. She watched me pull the net.

"Something distracting you?" I said, lifting a dozen fish over the roller.

"Not at all."

"Just want to make sure your head's in the game."

"Don't worry about me." She was breathing hard now. "Let me know if I need to cover up."

We worked frantically on the tangled, panicky mess of fish in front of us. Joe held the net under his boot as he threw fish from the deck into the holds with one hand.

"Cover what up?" I asked.

"I think you know."

"Do you work for Satan, or are you just under his influence?"

She threw a salmon right into my chest. "Oops, that one got away from me."

"If you start throwing fish, you're going to regret it."

"The devil made me do it."

I heard Joe chuckle. Realizing, of course, that we were not alone, Shenan and I temporarily bit our tongues. Besides, there was too much work to do. Halfway through the second shackle, I grew disheartened at the fact that we were only halfway. I needed a break. I needed a drink. My lungs burned. My forearms cramped, but I couldn't stop. The longer we waited, the heavier the net became.

Minutes later, Shenan turned backward and bent over to extricate a low-hanging fish. I took a seven-pounder by the tail and slapped it across her bottom. She put her hand on the boat to catch herself from tumbling forward. Turning abruptly, she pursed her lips and grimaced.

"I'm sorry," I said. "That actually was the devil."

She picked up a squirming salmon by the tail. "Okay, you two," Joe said, placing his hand on Shenan's forearm before she assaulted me with the fish. She dropped it, then attacked the net. By now, we were completely covered in scales and slime. Of all the days to not wear our coats, I thought.

We struggled our way through the last shackle. It was an unbelievable haul—probably twenty percent of our entire season. Once the net lay in a pile on the deck, we sat on the fish holds to catch our breath. We could have put the net out again, but Joe must have known we needed a break. Besides, with so many fish left on the deck, we didn't know if the boat could hold more without sinking precariously low in the water. After a quick drink, we picked the remaining salmon off the deck and threw them into the holds. They were completely full.

"It's only eleven o'clock," Shenan said. "We could let out one shackle, couldn't we?"

"Are you kidding me?" I said. "The boat's full and I'm . . ." I paused.

"You're what?"

"Tired."

"So am I, but it's only one shackle."

I looked at Joe.

"It's up to you guys. We can fill the deck. This is the last hour."

"Sure," I said, standing again. "Let 'er roll."

Shenan cast the net out again, this time paying out only one shackle. That way, we didn't have to worry about catching too many fish. We were still in the middle of a large school. In twenty minutes, we hauled her in. By the time we were done, we not only filled the holds, but we also filled the picking area up to our knees. I replaced

JOSHUA KEIL

the cover on the aft hold and laid down to rest. The boat
sat low in the water. "We'd better unload this before the
weather picks up," Joe said. "Then we can go to town to
shower and eat."

"That sounds wonderful," I said. Joe pushed the
throttle forward and pointed the bow toward Dillingham.

I glanced at Shenan. She had unbuckled the bib of
her slickers and lowered it to the top of her jeans. Soaking
wet, she lay on her back sprawled out on the net in her
torso-hugging tank top, covered in scales, blood, and
slime. Her eyes were closed. She looked exhausted but
happy. I forced myself to turn away from her. A line of
half a dozen seagulls followed us like we were the lead
bird on a long migration. I felt I could almost touch the
closest one. As I lay listening to the hum of the motor
not far below me, it sent vibrations throughout the boat,
through the fish holds, and the thick pile of net beneath
my head. I thought about what I would do with our free
time in town. The shower would feel heavenly. A meal
at the bar would taste superb. I also decided to look at the
boat for sale. I had grown more confident as a fisherman,
and Shenan had been right—this was the only way to
make a living. And no matter what transpired in town,

I determined that I would do anything to get back into Shenan's good graces.

# Chapter 10

# Cannery Girl

I returned to the cabin today after a long and frustrating search. The helicopter and tranquilizing team from Anchorage have been delayed for several days by bad weather, and the cauldron that is the village of Pedro Bay has started to boil. While doing an aerial survey this morning, I spotted a brown bear lying on the shores of Lake Iliamna. After landing in the lake to investigate, I approached the carcass with a loaded pistol and found it dead. I removed my green outfitters hat—one that I have had for more than forty-five years—and held it against my chest. It was a female, a sow, who had been shot two times with a rifle, probably at least two days before. I took hair samples and pictures.

Whoever did it, they did it illegally. It was out of season, no one had reported it to me, and no one had attempted to salvage the hide with skull and claws attached, which is mandatory even in cases of self-defense.

I returned to the village and made inquiries. There is little more than a few dozen people in town, so questioning them does not take long. Everyone claimed they had no idea who shot the bear. They wondered if someone from another town was to blame, or a tourist from the Lower Forty-Eight. They rightly pointed out that anyone could have landed a plane and shot the bear and flown to any other part of Alaska.

The one common refrain I heard was that perhaps this was the man-killing bear that killed the dentist. Perhaps she had tried to attack another person and they acted in self-defense. I pointed out that even if that was the case, such an act requires immediate notification to the state. Some suggested that perhaps the dentist had shot the bear before he died and that the wounded bear wandered for miles before dying on the lakeshore. While these scenarios do not quite jibe with my gut, I cannot rule them out. Regardless, I now have DNA from bear fur found on the dead fisherman and the dead bear from the lake. Time will soon tell whether they are one and the same.

But I doubt it. More than likely, the death of the dentist was just an excuse to go on a power trip. My plan is to return to the carcass tomorrow to recover some bullets for forensic analysis, then fly all the samples to Anchorage, along with the hide. But I will have to return quickly, barring good weather, for my presence is needed to prevent more acts like this. I figure the black wolf is also vulnerable so long as she remains in the vicinity. While making rounds with the villagers today, I cautioned them to be patient, reminded them of the consequences of illegally shooting game, and instructed them to come to me with new information.

"But what about the bear?" one woman asked me.

"The dead one?"

"No, the man-killer. He's still on the loose, isn't he?"

"Presumably, yes. But as soon as the helicopter gets here, we will tranquilize several animals. We'll find him."

"Let's pray he doesn't attack anyone else before then."

"If no one ventures into the woods alone, there shouldn't be any problems."

\*\*\*

By the time we arrived at the small boat harbor in Dillingham most of the fishing boats had already tied up to the pier. Either from sheer boredom or unlucky fishing, they had already quit for the day.

The crew of the *Nereid* had other reasons to go to town early. We found Phillip and Steve deep in the engine hold covered in grease. Engine parts lay strewn about the place. Phillip said that the *Nereid*'s engine had been misfiring and running poorly. The few mechanics in town were swamped and Phillip didn't have time to wait. He and Steve dove into the engine to discover the cause of the misfire. From the looks of the boxes strewn around, Phillip placed his hope in brand new spark plugs and wires.

"Are you gonna be alright, Uncle Phillip?" Shenan asked.

"I think so. We'll get her back together by tomorrow and see how she fares. I'd like to salvage as much of the season as possible."

"You guys need any help?" I asked.

Phillip said they didn't, to my relief. "As you can see, we can't fit more people around this thing anyway." They had already removed one of the engine's heads and were in the guts of the beast. Glad to hear we would not be drafted to fight the iron monster, the three of us from the *Mikilak* made plans. We would shower at the cannery, restock our grub at the B&C Commercial Company and finish the night with a meal at the Sea Tavern. I told Joe I first wanted to look at the salmon-colored boat for sale in the boatyard if he and Shenan didn't mind waiting forty-five minutes.

He nodded.

Shenan opened her mouth to speak, but Joe beat her to it. "Shenan and I will carry the trash out."

She glanced at his cast. "Right," she said, then turned to me. "Just make sure you tell us what you think of the boat."

We had tied ourselves to the *Nereid*, who in turn was tied to three other boats. Only one boat, the closest to the pier, was secured to anything solid while the rest of us clung to her like a string of pearls. I had to climb over four boats to get to the pier.

I walked the muddy gravel road to the boatyard. A dozen boats stood on stilts, unused for a variety of reasons—replaced by a new boat, broken down, or simply crewless. I walked up to the boat with the *For Sale* sign in the window. It appeared to be nearly new. Made of fiberglass, it was much more modern than the old, wooden *Mikilak.* And it was big—so big that its bow was "clipped" to prevent it from exceeding the length limit. This gave it a bull nosed appearance, ready to take on the ocean and all her wrath.

The sign said, "Inquire with manager," so I made my way to the building. I found a man who grudgingly left his office to show me the boat. We grabbed a ladder nearby and placed it against her gunnel far up in the air. I climbed aboard and the man followed.

"So, you're looking to buy a boat for yourself, huh?"

"I'm thinking about it."

"Who'dya say you fish with?"

"Joe Nukusuk." I prided myself in knowing his real name.

"Who's that?"

"Nushagak Joe."

"Oh, Nushagak Joe," he said, scratching the stubble on his chin. "I hear you guys have been havin' a real good season."

"Not too bad."

"If you're ready to skipper your own boat, this one's real nice—real clean and modern."

I surveyed the boat carefully. It was about the size and age of the *Nereid* and was similar in many respects. Yet, it was even larger than Phillip's boat. It could hold at least twenty percent more fish.

We examined the engine. "Does it run?" I asked.

"Don't see why not. It ran last year."

"Who's the owner?"

"A man in Anchorage. Decided to get out of fishing two seasons ago. He got a real job up there and has been trying to sell this thing ever since."

"Do many people come looking at it?"

"Not too many. Just a few in the off-season. Everyone's fishin' now. You're the first in a few months. I expect there'll be more when the season's over, but don't know with the bad season and all."

"Probably true," I said as I went into the cabin. It was big and spacious and had a modern galley. Between it and the berthing compartment, there was a tiny closet with a pump toilet. I imagined Shenan would love that. I descended further into the berthing space. There were two bunks on either side, their feet joining at the bow. They doubled as couches. What's more, they had thick foam mattresses, another thing that Shenan would appreciate right now. Then the man pulled a small shelf with a cushion on it out of the locker and placed it between the two bunks. With the centerpiece installed, the two bunks become one large bed—almost a real bed, albeit triangle-shaped.

"For the extra sleeping space if you need it," he said, returning the shelf to the locker. "So, what do you think?"

"I'm real interested. I might see you back here in a few weeks."

In truth, I planned to come back that very night.

I left the boatyard in high spirits. I immediately pictured Shenan in the boat with me. I pictured the triangle bed and her turning it into a homey place. I then imagined her putting a statue of the Buddha on the shelf near the bed. The fact remained—we were two different people, and quite possibly, she still hated me.

Back on the *Mikilak*, I found Joe and Shenan eating a small lunch. We ate Pilot crackers with peanut butter and jelly to hold us till dinner. I gave a good report of the boat. Shenan seemed very interested and encouraged me to pursue it. After cleaning up, we packed clean clothes into bags, locked up the *Mikilak*, and set out toward the hot showers of the cannery.

Many fishermen roved the town of Dillingham that day. Dillingham was probably like most Alaskan towns back then—all swarming with men working hard, making money, funneling into the little towns, hoping beyond hope that the lights they saw in the distance indicated the presence of women. The red-light districts that boomed across Alaska a half century earlier had technically disappeared, but the need was still there. There was a persistent rumor that hundreds of college girls from across the country had come to work in the canneries, meet men, and have some adventure, but they rarely materialized. More often than not, there were few women to be found. After working themselves up dreaming of the cannery girls, the men congregated like wolves in the street. The tension usually expressed itself in drunkenness and violence.

By the time Joe, Shenan and I went ashore, many of the roughnecks stumbled drunkenly about the streets. They passed us and gawked. Shenan elicited a few whistles along the way, but she was adept at ignoring them. I saw the familiar cannery in the distance, a corrugated metal building with rust stains sliding down its walls. We found the door marked: "Showers. Cannery workers and boat crews only!"

"Is this our cannery?" Shenan asked.

"Yep," I said, warily scanning the area. "We've provided more to their bottom dollar than most boats this season. We've earned this."

"They'd better be hot," she said, "my lungs need a good steaming."

Opening the door, we entered a long room with shower stalls lining the left side of the room and benches to the right. There were clothes thrown over many of the benches and steam rose from several stalls. Shenan looked at me with muted horror. "Are there no women's showers?"

"You're looking at 'em," I said. "You obviously should undress in the stall."

"Obviously," she said, her eyes darting around the room.

We walked past one stall where a man's hairy legs showed beneath the curtain from the calf down. A naked old man toweled himself in the corner.

"You don't do this at the University of Virginia?"

"Shut up." I felt her walking nearer to me. "You're going to be right next to me, right?"

"In the shower?"

"No, you perv. Outside."

"Yeah, I'll stay close."

The showers on the ends were taken, so we settled for open ones in the middle. Joe put his bag on a bench near the showers and started to undress, much to Shenan's horror. She turned away looking as casual as possible.

"Don't get that cast wet," I told Joe.

"I have a plan," he said, wrapping it in a plastic bag.

Shenan gathered things from her bag. "Should I hand my clothes out to you?"

"I would just drape them over the top. I'll wait for you to get in. Then I'll take a quick shower and get out before you."

"Do you think those curtain rods are solid?" she said, trying not to make eye contact with any of the men in the room. All her talk of the fishermen having to control themselves had dissipated.

"They look pretty sturdy."

I watched as she draped a small blue dress over the curtain rod. The paisley shapes on it swam around each other in blue and purple hues like microscopic beings in a primordial ocean. She removed her shoes and socks, stepped into the shower and pulled the curtain. I sat on the bench and waited. She threw her jeans, tank-top and bandana over the rack. Her slim calves showed beneath the curtain. The faucet wheel squeaked, and steam poured from the stall. She coughed. I looked around and saw men in various stages of undress, some toweling their hair, all clueing into the female voice that coughed profusely. They were either drawn by the sound of a female or alarmed by a fear of tuberculosis.

One of her calves disappeared. I imagined she was shaving her leg, resting her foot on the rough concrete wall. I watched and imagined more and decided it was time to take my shower. I walked to the stall next to Shenan's, clinching my towel around my waist.

Despite dreaming of a hot shower all day, I turned on the cold water, and soaped down immediately, knowing I had to be quick. Shenan coughed something up—apparently quite a bit—and was now spitting in the drain. I finally arrived at a state where I could turn on the warm water.

"Are you okay?" I said loudly, trying to cast my voice to the shower next to me.

"Yeah, I'm just not used to the steam." Her muffled voice sounded normal, which reassured me. Still, I decided I would convince her to go to a doctor to see if she needed antibiotics.

As I shaved in the shower without the aid of a mirror, I heard two new voices in the room. Drunk, laughing voices. Peeking outside, I saw two men in the back of the room pointing at Shenan's stall. One of them said something about a cannery girl. It was only then that a thought that had been teasing me all day fully dawned on me. There was a creature meeting the exact description of a fabled cannery girl in the stall next to mine—a beautiful young undergrad who came to Alaska looking for adventure. She fit the bill in all respects except that she worked for a boat rather than a cannery. A thousand men across the region were now looking for cannery girls and she might be the only real one. I finished shaving and grabbed my towel. I exited the stall and dressed, then sat on the bench between the gawking men and Shenan.

They talked quietly behind me. "Who the hell is she?" one of them said.

"Judging by those purple panties, I'd like to find out." Shenan stood on her tiptoes. Her hand appeared above the curtain to aim the water nozzle.

"My, my, my," I heard the other say. "I hope we get a peek."

"Maybe if someone took her clothes and put them on the bench, she'd have no choice but to come out."

The other one chuckled. "No one ever got hurt by looking."

I stood and turned to them, jerking a thumb toward the door. "You guys had better move along."

One of them was large with shaggy hair, the other a smaller man with a long, gray-streaked beard. They were both several years older than me.

"What are you talking about?" the big man said.

"You can't harass a woman like that. You need to move along."

"Take it easy. We didn't know she was with you."

"Well, she is."

"Is she from the cannery?"

I shrugged.

"It was a simple question," the man with the beard said.

It was clear that he wanted to confirm the existence of cannery girls. It must have been important to know they were real.

"She doesn't work at the cannery. She works on a boat. She's a puller."

He looked surprised, then nodded his head as the two shuffled to the other end of the room.

Joe exited the shower and dressed clumsily with one arm. We waited for Shenan a few minutes more. I found myself looking over my shoulder now.

Finally, loud faucet squeaks announced the end of her long shower. I watched as the towel disappeared over the curtain rod, then her underwear followed by her dress. She came out drying her hair, demurely looking around the room, standing in an unbelievably small dress.

"Do you have pants?" I asked.

She giggled. "No, Jim, this is a gypsy dress." She momentarily made eye contact with the rude men on the other end of the room.

I couldn't believe she planned to wear that outfit in town. While the sleeves were long and flowing, the dress had no straps and left her shoulders completely exposed, showing the tan lines from her bib overalls. What's worse, the uneven hem reached only halfway down her long, tan thighs, exposing nearly the full extent of her legs.

"Sorry I was so long in there." She buckled a thick belt around her small waist. "That was heavenly."

"You sound sick," Joe said. "We should take you to a doctor."

"I was thinking the same thing," I said.

"It was just my asthma. I already have medicine— you've seen it." She pulled leather boots from her bag and zipped them up along her calves, then started brushing her hair. Her eyes darted around the room again then rested on me. "I appreciate your concern, but the only thing I want right now is to get out of here." As we gathered our things and headed to the door, she asked, "Jim, who were you talking to?"

"Just some fisherman," I said, opening the door for Shenan. I turned to see all the men in the shower room watching us leave. "Just small talk."

We stepped into the sunlight. The day was almost warm, but not quite. Shenan put a thin, navy sweater over her bare shoulders, then put her backpack over that. She put a broad yellow bandana over her hair and large sunglasses on. She looked like a fashion model. I felt like a man walking around with a bag that said "money" on the side. The encounter with the fishermen put me on edge, and I was even more worried because I knew I was going to leave Shenan and Joe for a while.

"Shenan," I said, "I think the next time we come to town, you should wear something a little more modest."

"That was rather judgmental. Is that for my sake, or for yours?"

"For your sake. And for the sake of all the men."

"I don't have to change the way I dress because of what men think."

"Shenan, when you ask men to control themselves, it doesn't mean you have to make it as hard as possible. It's a two-way street, you know."

"Are you saying rape is a two-way street?"

"What?"

"I understand you perfectly, Jim. In the future I will do my best not to tempt you."

"I'm not talking about me."

"Then who are you talking about?"

"The fishermen!" I yelled. My outburst drew a look from a grizzled man carrying a box of groceries. I lowered my voice. "I already said that. You can talk all you want about what men should or should not do, but that doesn't necessarily affect what they will do."

She pursed her lips like she was thinking, then grinned. "I didn't know this dress was going to be such a problem for you."

I rubbed the bridge of my nose. "Shenan, if you're that naïve, then never mind."

She looked at me like I might have gotten through to her but said nothing. And neither did I. Besides, I had to go.

"Joe," I said, "would you and Shenan be able to get the groceries on your own?"

"Yes."

"Then if you don't mind, I need to go back to the boatyard to take another look around the boat."

Shenan looked at me curiously. "Again?"

"Yes."

Joe said, "See you back at the boat."

"It won't take long."

I veered in the opposite direction from Shenan and Joe, then glanced back. Shenan looked worried about seeing me go. *Serves her right*, I thought. *She could stand to have a little bit more fear.*

I was a little unsure of what I was doing, but her forlorn face fired me with resolve. I ran back to the *Mikilak* and grabbed a large duffle bag. I folded it neatly under my arm and returned to the boatyard, wishing it was darker. *Damn the long summer days,* I thought. I didn't like sneaking around—it wasn't my nature. Fifteen minutes later, mission accomplished, I was back at the

*Mikilak.* I stowed the duffle bag on my rack and walked toward the store, not wanting to leave the other two alone for long.

I found them coming down the hill. I relieved Shenan of a large cardboard box full of heavy grocery items, mostly cans, but she kept a bag that she insisted on carrying. Joe and I followed her across all four boats. It was absurd watching Shenan step from boat to boat in that tiny blue dress. She certainly revealed more than just her middle thighs at times. As she crossed the boats, I wondered if fishermen watched from portholes below like hellions looking up toward the heavens. While unloading the groceries, she asked what I had been doing.

"I'll tell you later," I said. "First, it's time to blow off a little steam."

# Chapter 11

# The Sea Tavern

After stowing the groceries, we walked up the dirt road to the Sea Tavern. Along the way, Shenan turned the head of every man we passed.

We sat at a booth in the corner and waited for the waitress, the kind of woman one would expect to find in Bristol Bay—a middle-aged married woman with a rough countenance. Even she looked at Shenan with a strange expression. I couldn't blame her. The huge sunglasses were especially out of place.

All three of us ordered cheeseburgers. Shenan ordered hers without onions. I did the same, even though I love onions.

"And to drink?" the waitress asked.

"I'll have a beer," Shenan said. "How 'bout you guys?"

"Just water tonight," Joe said.

"C'mon, Joe, let's celebrate the big haul today."

Shenan unknowingly made two crucial mistakes—asking an alcoholic to drink and bragging about good-luck fishing in a bad-luck town. I glared at her, but she didn't understand. "Geez, Jim, why are you so afraid of fun?"

"I'm already having fun."

"It doesn't sound like it."

"I'll explain it to you later."

"You're right," Joe said, "we need to celebrate." He ordered a beer and unknowingly proved my point.

I ordered a Coke and the waitress left. Shenan unfolded her napkin in her lap. "Jim, you want to know my opinion?"

"Not really."

"You need to loosen up."

"And you call me the judgmental one?"

"Yes, you do an excellent job trying to make people around you feel bad about themselves. Just because you're such an old fuddy-duddy doesn't mean you have to make everyone else feel that way."

"I'm not as strait-laced as you think."

"Yeah, right."

"I enjoy a beer as much as the next man. I just gave it up, that's all."

"Why?"

"Because it destroys people's lives." I wanted to nod at Joe but couldn't.

"Jesus turned water into wine, didn't he?" Shenan asked. "Didn't he drink wine at the Last Supper? The Bible doesn't say not to drink, Jim. In fact, it just says not to drink *in excess*. Everything in moderation, Jim. That's what the Buddha says, and that's what the Bible says."

Joe said, "Have a drink, Jim. You deserve one."

I was exasperated—with both of them. Apparently, Joe did not appreciate that I was trying to support him.

"You two are incorrigible," I said. Joe smiled, and for some reason, I decided to lighten up for his sake. "I imagine that if they had cheeseburgers in Galilee, Jesus would have turned the water into beer."

Shenan raised her empty glass in the air. "Well said, Jim." She turned to the waitress who was just bringing our drinks. "One more beer, please."

When the waitress left, Shenan excused herself to use the ladies' room, saying she was going to take advantage of that as much as possible while ashore. A minute later, the waitress returned with my beer. She asked the two of us how the fishing was going. We told her it was going well enough, downplaying the "big haul" that Shenan alluded to earlier. I could tell the waitress was now in a chatty mood, but the bar was filling up with ruffians of every shape and appearance. I wondered what was taking Shenan so long.

Finally, she strode toward us, a newspaper in hand. She plopped it on the table in front of me. "This is what I'm talking about!" she said fingering a small headline. *Ice Highway to Alaska's North Stirs Concern for Arctic Ecology – Winter Road to Oil Fields Appears Now as Muddy Gouge Across the Tundra—Danger to Wildlife Feared.*

"Read the whole thing."

I unfolded the paper and read it aloud so Joe could hear. It was a syndicated column from the New York Times, which discussed the "Walter J. Hickel Ice Highway" that had been built to supply the new oil fields in Prudhoe Bay. The reporter detailed how the highway might disrupt the tundra, the thousands of 55-gallon drums scattered across the area, and the proposed pipeline to carry oil from Prudhoe Bay to the port of Valdez. The article cited concerns that the pipeline would hinder the migration of the caribou herds now numbering nearly half a million. It further discussed the possible damage from a break in the line in some distant mountain valley or in the ocean near Valdez. Finally, it mentioned the only alternative—an oil tanker on the East Coast that had been converted into an icebreaker. It was called the *SS Manhattan* and would try to break through the Northwest Passage that very summer to prove that North Slope oil could be carried by icebreaking oil tankers rather than a pipeline.

I was captivated by the notion of steaming the Northwest Passage. I had read about the explorers who had tried to find a northern sea route from the Atlantic to the Pacific. After a few hundred years of searching, they found it along Canada's northern coasts, but it was perpetually locked in ice, even through the summer, and therefore impassable.

When I placed the paper down, Shenan said, "This is the development I'm talking about." She placed her finger on the paper again. "Are they going to turn Alaska into an industrial waste dump?"

I rubbed my jaw, which felt strangely smooth after the shower and shave. The beers arrived and I waited for the waitress to leave. "We don't know that all of those things are going to happen."

"It doesn't sound good," she said.

Joe remained silent, furrowing his brow as he took the paper from me and looked it over.

"It's all speculation," I said. "It just says there are *worries* about the tundra and the caribou and the safety of the pipe. And besides, they may never build it. The icebreaker might get the oil to the East Coast and to the oil-hungry Virginians."

She pursed her lips and darted her eyes at me. I was trying to lighten the mood, but it didn't work. She backed off, spreading the napkin on her lap again. "I'm just saying that someday the whole world is going to be an industrial site at the rate we're going."

I raised my beer in the air. "To Alaska!" I said. "May she ever be an unpolluted frontier."

Shenan smiled again. She and Joe raised their glasses to mine.

"To Alaska!" they said in unison.

There is nothing like the absence of comforts to make simple things wonderful. After a week with no shower and nothing but bad food, the luxuries of town spoiled us. The beer tasted better than ever. The cheeseburger reminded me how good food could be. Between the new boat, my seemingly lucrative future, Shenan's hazel eyes, the delicious food, the alcohol, and good company, I lived in a perfect moment. We ordered a second round. Shenan talked and giggled. Without asking, she reached across the table to steal the pickles off my plate. The paisley shapes on her dress swam in the blue ocean of the fabric. I was dizzy with alcohol, and with happiness.

My lust for life was held in check only by the constant stares from the crowd of roughnecks. They eyeballed Shenan like a cheeseburger dropped into a life raft of starving men. With impunity, they gawked at her legs under the booth. Eventually, I asked Shenan to scoot in, then switched sides, shielding her to the inside. Out of the corner of my eye, I caught the threatening stares of many of the sourdoughs, their grizzled beards hardly concealing their contempt. Shenan looked at me and smiled. "Decided you wanted closer company?"

"I'm just tired of those guys staring at you."

"Is that all?"

"And I don't mind close company."

We ordered more beer and talked and laughed for quite some time. Joe was silent, like usual, but smiled often. He seemed to enjoy having Shenan around as much as I did, or almost as much. I realized what a positive influence she had been on the boat. I wondered if Joe was glad his only choice for a deck hand was a girl.

When the jukebox started to play rock 'n roll, Shenan's eyes lit up. "Let's dance!"

"I'm not going to dance to rock 'n roll."

"Oh, c'mon. Don't tell me you don't dance."

"Of course I dance. I'm excellent at foxtrot and waltz and…" She giggled again and motioned me out of the booth. "No," I reiterated, "I don't know how to dance to this kind of music."

"Fine then," she said, "I'll dance by myself." She motioned me out of the booth. Afterward, I sat down and watched as she made her way to the jukebox and started snapping her fingers and swaying with the music on her own. "I *love* this song," she said. It was a man singing about a girl with brown eyes—a girl from the past and the memories they had together. I could see how a girl with brown eyes would love a song like that, even if Shenan's were closer to hazel. Shenan lifted her hands to her cheeks and sang along. One of the young fishermen came over and took her hand politely. She complied. For a few minutes they danced in front of one another. Men stood around and watched. More men filtered into the bar every minute. They gathered in a circle and watched. Another man cut in, obviously a little drunker. The crowd grew until it hindered my view.

When the song ended and another began, Shenan dashed back to our table, took a quick drink, and said, "Last chance, Jim. Will you just try one dance—for me?"

I reluctantly slid out of the booth. "Okay. For you."

She took my hand. On our way to the middle of the floor I was pleased to hear the song was more traditional than the other music. I put my hand on her hip and held her right hand high in the air. The song was called "Those Were the Days My Friend." It sounded Russian, and I could almost imagine that we were in Alaska back at the turn of the century during the Gold Rush, when the state was just a territory full of men from all over the world. The crowd of grizzled men that watched us probably looked little different than the men of those days. We swayed and twirled and tripped and laughed around the floor. Thirty men closed in and watched us, but all my attention was on Shenan—Shenandoah and her bright eyes and easy laugh. I didn't know if we were a couple, but it sure felt like we were.

When the song ended and a new one began, I felt a tap on my shoulder. I turned to find a middle-aged man with a thick moustache bowing comically with a twirl of his hand. "May I have this dance?" he asked in a gravelly voice. I turned to Shenan to gauge her thoughts. She shrugged and smiled, so I let him cut in.

Melting into the crowd of men, I made my way toward Joe who was standing in the back but remained close enough to see her. She and the man danced in front of each other. Every time he took her hand to spin her, she would just as quickly remove it.

After a minute or two, I heard the man ask, "You wanna party with us tonight?"

"No, thanks," she said.

"We have tequila and music."

"I'm not a big partier. I just love to dance."

She kept dancing, her hands high in the air, looking down at her own hips as they gyrated with the music, lifting her eyes occasionally to look at the other men, and sometimes at me. Her gypsy dress gave up trying to hide her curves. Shenan's hips picked up the fabric as she moved, revealing what was really at the top of all those legs—fullness, roundness, a revelation of womanhood that had been hidden behind the girly facade.

"We can dance on my boat, baby" another man said.

She ignored him.

Several men came to dance now. One took her hand and kissed it as they moved. "You're going home with somebody tonight, aren't you?"

"No," she said. "I'm going back to my boat."

I heard a few of them talking. "Let's take her down to Tiny's place," one of them said.

"You think she'll come?"

"With a few more beers she will."

I tried calculating how many beers she'd had— three, and I could tell that was enough to put her into the Bible's "drunken in excess" category.

An old man swayed up to her with two shots of tequila and handed one over. "For you, m'lady." She looked at it with some disgust as she took it in her hand. "You're the most beautiful woman I've ever seen," he said. She smiled. He tapped his glass to hers. "To the most beautiful woman in the whole world." He swallowed. After a moment's hesitation, Shenan pitched hers back as well. She coughed a little, looking young again in her childish dress. I felt the situation moving from harmless fun to reckless behavior.

One of the fishermen close to me said, "That'll help."

"Yep," said another.

"How old do you think she is?"

"Old enough."

I turned to Joe. "I think we should leave."

He nodded.

The man who gave her the shot put his arm around her waist and danced close to her. I cut through the crowd. "Shenan, it's time to go."

Some of the men booed collectively.

"Why, Jim?" she said, slurring her words. "Are you jealous?"

"I just think we should leave."

She looked at her watch. "It's only nine thirty. Are you *sure* you're not jealous?"

"Yes, I'm sure."

"I was hoping you came out here to dance more. Are you turning back into a stick-in-the-mud?"

"Somebody has to be one."

One man yelled out, "Let the lady do what she wants!"

Still dancing, Shenan looked at me. "Yeah, Jim, let the lady do what she wants."

The crowd cheered, which made her smile.

"C'mon, Jim!" one of them yelled mockingly.

"Leave her alone!" said another. A new man brought another shot of tequila. He placed it in her hand.

"Shenan," I said as serious as I could, "I would love to dance more, but it's getting late." She looked at the shot glass. "Please don't drink that," I said.

Fire shot from her eyes as she grabbed the glass and downed it. She handed it back to the man and cocked an eyebrow in my direction. The crowd of men catcalled and cheered.

"Okay, that's it," I said. "It's time someone taught you a lesson." The men cheered again, which seemed to confuse Shenan. They had been cheering for her, but I think they liked the idea of someone teaching her a lesson.

I took her by the forearm to lead her away, but she refused to move. Bending her long legs and leaning back, she said, "Let go of me!"

"No, you are in danger," I said, being as explicit as I could be. She slapped my arm with her free hand. The crowd cheered. Realizing there was only one way out of this, I picked her up and threw her over my shoulder. That wasn't the smartest maneuver considering the length of her dress and this drew the greatest hollers yet. Shenan yelled for me to put her down and pounded on my back as I strode quickly toward the door. Some of the men cheered me on like a warrior about to partake of his spoils, but others booed and scowled. Some of the men acted like they were going to intervene until I gave them a hard look. I only prayed that Shenan would not call for help. If she did, I knew the miscreants would be more than happy to rescue her.

But she didn't.

With Shenan over my shoulder, still beating on my back, I marched quickly outside. In the cool night air, we made our way around a corner and disappeared into an alley. I felt a little safer, but I couldn't wait to put more distance between us and that bar.

# Chapter 12

# The Treasure in the Boat

Finn Nickolai checked on me today. He is worried that the hullabaloo surrounding the death of the dentist will derail my plans to speak at the rally.

"Don't forget about Saturday night," he said.

"What day is today?"

"Tuesday."

"I have to fly the bear samples to Anchorage, but I'll be back today or tomorrow. I plan to be there."

Finn opened a brown paper bag. "You want a donut?"

"Sure."

"Have you decided what to speak about?"

"Many things," I said, swallowing my first bite. "I'm definitely telling them what I saw in the Lower Forty-Eight. That's the main thing. I had no idea there was something like that in America."

"Worse than you expected?"

"Yes. But I also want to talk about the McNeil River."

"Ah. The road will be very close."

"And that's a big problem."

"The noise?"

"No, the food. You know how animals are. The moment they associate humans with food they turn into problem animals."

"You think somebody fed this bear?"

"I don't know. It may have been something else— lack of food, old age, injury, self-defense."

"You think he is a McNeil River bear?"

"Possibly."

Finn's question is important. Pedro Bay is only fifty miles from what is arguably the greatest wildlife viewing station in the world—the McNeil River State Game Sanctuary and Refuge. Pictures of the waterfalls, where dozens of brown bears gather to catch salmon, are world famous. In my mind, the refuge is the paragon of proper game management. Only ten people can observe the bears at a time, and they are absolutely forbidden to leave food waste. These strenuous rules have allowed thousands of people to observe one of the world's largest predators up close without a single injury to humans in more than fifty years of existence. This is especially phenomenal considering nearly four people are hospitalized in Alaska every year due to bear attacks, and roughly one bear-related death occurs every other year. Even these numbers are extremely low. Far more people are hospitalized from dog bites and bicycling injuries. Still, the McNeil River Sanctuary is especially safe. And it is made possible by the fact that the bears only interact with humans under very controlled conditions.

"What makes you think they'll get fed?" Finn asked with a mouthful of donut.

"The haul rode passes within fifteen miles of the refuge. The bears who gather at the falls traverse that territory all the time. If the mine is built, those bears will come into contact with humans outside of the carefully controlled conditions. They will have close encounters with trucks. They may eat food discarded by truck drivers or pipeline workers. The bears would have all sorts of new interactions. And if there's an attack at the McNeil

River—like the one here—everything's going to change. Someday we may speak of the time when people could stand within a few feet of brown bears—the time before the dynamic between humans and bears changed forever."

"You are starting to get it, Jim," Finn said, as if his thinking was already years ahead of mine. "Will you speak about the McNeil River?"

"I plan to."

"And what about Bristol Bay?"

"What about it?"

"Have you been writing?"

"Yes." I tapped the laptop on the table. "I've written a great deal."

"Good," he said, wadding up the brown paper bag, "I can't wait to read it."

I feel like a pawn in his hands, but that's okay. Finn Nickolai is playing chess with the big boys, and he needs all the help he can get.

*** 

I carried Shenan twenty-five yards before I placed her leather boots on the ground. Regaining her feet, she slapped my cheek, folded her arms, then plodded off toward the harbor.

"I can't believe you picked me up in this dress!"

"I can't believe you wore that ridiculous dress to begin with."

She turned abruptly. "What's wrong with it? Don't you like it?" Her eyes moistened.

"Yes, I like your dress, but—"

"Thank you. Was that so hard to say?"

"No, it wasn't hard. I was—"

"You've been putting it down all day."

"I wasn't putting it down. I like your dress. You look beautiful in it. I only meant it was ridiculous because we're in the wilds of Alaska for God's sake. I just thought it was dangerous."

She turned and walked toward the water. Joe followed.

"Dangerous? Don't you think you're being a bit dramatic?"

"No."

"And I don't appreciate you carrying me out of there," she said, her voice slurring from the alcohol. "That was completely unnecessary."

"Don't you get it? Don't you know what those guys were trying to do?"

"They were trying to have a good time."

"Exactly, but your idea of a good time and their idea of a good time are completely different. Every one of them was planning to get you drunk and take you some place where they could have their way with you."

She looked over at Joe who nodded his head. "Sometimes this place isn't safe for women," he said.

I could see in her face that she started to believe us, and I supposed it was a frightening realization. She turned again, but this time walked slowly toward the pier, just a dejected drunk girl.

"Men are such pigs," she said. "I mean, they really are animals."

"Not all of them," Joe said as we plodded toward the harbor behind her.

"You're right, Joe," she said, slowing down to take his arm. She steadied herself by leaning against him. "I know you aren't."

Reaching the harbor, Shenan began the arduous task of climbing over the four boats in our line. She stumbled in her high leather boots as she stepped over nets and straddled the gunnels. She refused my help but accepted it from Joe. She was practically in his arms by the halfway point. The *Nereid*'s engine hold remained open, but Phillip and Steve were not on the boat. Shenan went to the *Mikilak* first to "use the bucket" while Joe and I waited on the *Nereid*. With our backs to the *Mikilak* I heard her dump the bucket's contents overboard. Then, speaking loudly in my direction, "You could have at least waited for me to use a real bathroom one last time."

"Are you done?"

"Yes."

Joe and I climbed onto the *Mikilak* while Shenan lowered the bucket by its rope to rinse it. After returning the bucket to the deck, she remained at the gunnel and bent down toward the water to wash her hands, then paused. "I'm not feeling well."

"I believe it."

"I should have said no to the tequila."

I didn't say anything. After washing her hands, she got up slowly and went to the pilot house to change her clothes. Once she closed the hatch of the berthing compartment, I took the opportunity to pee in the water, then washed my hands and lounged on the deck with Joe. A minute later, she opened the door wearing white long johns that were a little too big for her.

"Get new pajamas?" I asked.

"Yes," she said, "but they only had men's long underwear."

"It looks fine," I said, "and I have something else for you." Entering the berthing compartment near her, I pulled the duffle bag off my rack and revealed the object of my covert operation. Removing one of the long, thick cushions from the salmon-colored boat, I unrolled it and placed it on the bench. "I got this for you at the boatyard."

Her face looked genuinely touched. "Oh, Jim," she said, "thank you." I could smell the tequila on her breath. "Did it cost much?"

"No," I said, trying to adjust its position on the bench. It was a little too long and curled up the wall. It overhung the bench and left only a few inches for us to stand, but it made a soft bed. I laid her sleeping bag and pillow on it. "You looked really uncomfortable last night."

Shenan sat on it. "Mmm . . . This is so nice, Jim." She laid her head against the bulkhead and closed her eyes. "Thank you."

"And despite what happened tonight," I said, "I want to say thank you, too."

"For what?"

"For getting me to dance."

"For that?"

"You're right, I need to loosen up."

"You know what?" she asked.

"What?" I said, my heart beating with anticipation.

"I think I'm going to be sick." Her hand went to her mouth again. Her stomach lurched, but nothing came up. I quickly scooped her up and carried her to the deck. Just as I got her head over the side she vomited into the water. She lay face down across my lap with her hands on the gunnel and her chin on her hands. "Why does the boat have to move so much?"

"It won't move if we don't." Joe walked out on deck to check on us, which moved the boat, and Shenan vomited again. I held her hair and rubbed the back of her new long johns.

Joe handed me a towel, which I used to wipe her mouth. "Need anything else?" he asked.

"For the boat not to move," she said weakly. He crept back to the cabin like he was sneaking away.

"Beer before liquor, never sicker," she said when he was gone.

"What's that?"

"An expression that I should pay more attention to." Still hunched over my lap, she laid her cheek on her hands, looking like she felt a little better, then started to sing the song we had danced to. *"We'd live the life we'd choose; We'd fight and never lose. Those were the days. Yes, those were the days."* Returning to her normal voice, she said, "Sorry I slapped you."

"It's okay."

"And you're right—those guys totally would have tried things."

"I thought you didn't want anyone to protect your honor."

"How do I know you're not doing the same thing as those men? Aren't you going to try anything?"

"Not when you're drunk."

"Wow, they really do exist."

"What?"

"Gentlemen." Before I could say anything, she sat up and said, "I think I'm ready to go to my rack."

"Do you want me to carry you?"

"Sure."

For the third time that night, I lifted her in my arms. The berthing door was open. I squeezed through the narrow space and laid her in her sleeping bag on the large, soft cushion. She squeezed my hand. "Thank you." She closed her eyes as I zipped the bag.

Joe, who rested in his bed with his back to us, said, "I think we'll leave in the morning. I think we should try Kvichak Bay."

"All right," I said. "Wake me up when it's time."

I crawled onto my hard, flat rack. I lay awake thinking about Shenan for several minutes. I thought about the thick foam cushion under her body. Somehow, it made my own rack feel softer and I drifted off.

\*\*\*

I hadn't been asleep for long when I awoke to the sound of footsteps on our boat. This wouldn't have been significant if we weren't the last boat in the line. I wondered if someone had tied onto the *Mikilak*, which would have made for an unusually long line, but I hadn't heard the bumps or felt the jarring of another vessel.

My confusion ended seconds later when I heard an unfamiliar voice from outside. "Cannery girl," a man said slowly and teasingly, "are you in there?" Ice pumped into my arteries. Many of the men at the Sea Tavern had seen Shenan with Joe, and they knew Joe and they knew his boat. Shenan was a treasure, and many fishermen knew where to find the "X" on the map.

I looked at Shenan to see if they roused her. She was dead asleep. I reached for my watch—we had only been asleep for an hour. I put on my pants and shirt.

I heard another voice. "Hey, Joe, are you in there? Steve told us the cannery girl was your deck hand. We want to invite you guys to a party."

I climbed down from my rack as quietly as I could and didn't bother with my boots. Joe stirred as well. The movement woke Shenan. She watched me step up to the main cabin.

"We know you're in there," the first voice said. I stepped outside where I found them standing on the aft fish hold balancing themselves on the upward pylons of the roller. The two men swerved more than the motion of the boat called for. The larger man stood near the back while his partner stood closer with a bottle in hand. I recognized at least one of them from the Sea Tavern. Surprise registered on their faces when they saw me.

"Have we got a problem?" I asked.

"Hey, man," the shorter man said. "There's no problem." He held out his hands, one still clutching the bottle. "We're just here to party with the cannery girl."

"I don't think she's interested."

The bigger man chimed in. "Why don't we just ask her?" I saw his eyes light up as he turned his attention behind me. I turned and saw Shenan's petite frame standing in her long johns near the hatch, her face hidden in the shadows. Joe passed her and stood beside me.

"Maybe she should speak for herself," the shorter man said, slurring his words as he spoke. "She seemed to be in a real party mood tonight until you hauled her away."

"She's not in a party mood now."

"Is that because you've already had your way with her?" the bigger man said, chuckling.

"No, and that wouldn't be any of your business."

"Good," the short man said, "then she's single."

"Hey, little lady," the big man called. "You wanna dance?"

"I'm not interested," Shenan said. I was surprised by the complete lack of fear in her voice. She spoke with composure, almost indifference.

"You heard her," I said. "You guys need to leave."

The man with the bottle stepped onto the fish hold right in front of me. Though he was much shorter, he towered over me from that position. I was more worried about the man behind him. "I think we'll stay here and party by ourselves," the man with the bottle said.

The bigger man stepped up behind his friend. "And when the lady feels like having a good time, we'll be waiting."

"No, you're leaving now," I said. I reached for the large man. Grabbing the front of his shirt in two fists, I dragged him across the boat and threw him over the opposite gunnel. Amidst a great deal of splashing and cursing, he swam toward the pier a short distance away. I turned to his friend but found that Joe already had him by the collar and was escorting him toward the *Nereid*.

The man stumbled over the side of the *Nereid*, nearly tumbling into her open engine hold. I watched him pass over a few of the other boats before I turned to Shenan. Her eyes wide, she clutched the door jamb.

Joe furrowed his brow. "Let's head to the Kvichak tonight. We'll fish there in the morning."

We were on the same page—both worrying that we might get more visitors, or that the same guys would return with friends.

"That sounds like a good idea." I glanced at the clock in the pilot house. It was a little past one o'clock in the morning. I knew that Kvichak Bay was a long way off. "How long will it take?"

"Maybe five hours."

"Ok," I said, "let's get started."

We checked the *Nereid* for signs of Phillip or Steve, but no one was aboard. Possibly, they were at the aforementioned party. If I had found Steve, I would have knocked his lights out for telling those guys where to find Shenan. Instead, I left a note on their hatch detailing where we were headed and telling Steve that he had better shut up about Shenan. We untied the *Mikilak* and Joe motored us out of the harbor. Once the bow turned toward open water, I told Joe I would take the first watch. Shenan asked if I was awake enough to pilot the boat. I said that I was and told her to get some sleep.

"Are you sure?" she asked.

"I'm sure. Besides, I didn't get that cushion for nothing."

"I'll take advantage of it." She placed her hand on my shoulder, stood on her tip toes, pulled me over, and kissed me on the cheek. "Thank you," she said. She turned and went down the few steps to the berthing compartment.

It was a pleasant night. The water pulsated with a slight chop. The *Mikilak* plowed through the waves, rolling gently, her engine hum varying slightly as she rode up and down the lazy swells. With one hand on the wheel, I pushed the berthing door open and saw Shenan fast asleep on the bench. The sight of her warmed me. She needed the sleep. It was a shame that she had been disturbed by those pigs. She was right, I thought, men are animals. The only difference between me and those other guys was that I tried hard not to be. I thought, then, that there was no intrinsic difference between a gentleman and a brute. It was simply a matter of self-control. I thought, too, that my self-control could not hold up much longer.

When my adrenaline faded, I struggled to stay awake. Lulled by the drone of the engine, I imagined salmon shooting beneath our boat and sea grass swaying in a foreign world fifty feet below. I buzzed from the beer and straddled the zone between sleep and wakefulness. Shenan's blue paisley dress danced into my thoughts, and the shapes on it swam through my mind like small ocean creatures. That was appropriate, I thought. Shenan was a sea-nymph if I ever saw one, and I was lucky to have found her. Most sailors never have a chance to see a sea nymph come ashore. I leaned over again and watched her. Dry and bundled up, she was caught firmly in our berthing compartment. I thought we should keep her.

*Wake up, Jim!*, my mind screamed at itself for the tenth time. I was far too tired. The only thing that kept me awake was the occasional putter of the old engine. In a way, I was glad the old workhorse had her quirks. It was as if she knew that an occasional stutter from the engine was enough to keep a fisherman on edge, and enough to prevent her soothing sound from putting the same person to sleep. I peered out over the dark ocean watching intently for any black shadow of a hazard. We were making good time—that I could tell. But even with the slight tailwind, I knew it would take a few more hours to get over to the Kvichak side.

Nearing three o'clock, the northern skies grew as dark as they would get. It was nice to stay up late, to see the night, to see the faint stars. I missed them. They reminded me of the winter I had spent at the Bible Camp. They reminded me of frost-covered trees and the mountains and the long, muffled periods of darkness. Those places seemed distant then—the Bible Camp, the Chickaloon River, and Castle Mountain, which loomed over them both. I missed the lakes and the trails and the horses. I grew tired of the Bay. I grew tired of the turbulent days and my shifting thoughts. I felt I needed to go into the mountains to find myself again. If I spent time alone, would I find that I was the same person? Was it too late? Then I realized I didn't want to go into the mountains alone. I wondered if I could take the sea nymph far from her natural element. I wanted to show her the long black nights, and the green auroras pirouetting in the sky. I wanted to walk through a snowy forest with her, our feet crunching in the snow. I wanted to hear the silence when we stopped to listen for animals in the forest. In my mind's eye, I watched her steamy breath in the moonlight as she listened, open-lipped, to the sound of a distant loon crying in the night. Then, still standing in the snow, she said, "Wake up, Jim," and I did, and redirected the boat to the proper heading.

Joe appeared in the berthing hatch and I realized how delirious my thoughts had become and how dangerously tired I was. He looked around in the darkness. Only one distant point of land was visible, but his familiarity with the Bay seemed to tell him where we were.

"Are you sure you've had enough sleep?"

"Yes. Now it's your turn."

I climbed down the two small steps. Shenan lay on her side, her hair now in a ponytail, her chest heaving gently in her new long johns. I wanted to crawl in behind her but climbed into my upper bunk instead. This time,

I lay awake for no more than a minute. I conjured up the thoughts of Shenan standing with me in the snow listening to the distant sound of the loon. I imagined we were on a quest to find the Loon. Shenan's eyes appeared extra golden in the blue light of the moon, and they sparkled from the excitement of the search. "This way," she whispered, pointing in the direction of the call. She took me by the hand and led me deep into the snow-laden trees.

# Chapter 13

# Wolves

I awoke to the sound of the engine throttling down. From experience, I guessed that Joe approached an anchorage. Through the portholes overhead, I saw a bright, overcast sky. I had slept for three hours after Joe replaced me at the helm. The berthing hatch was closed, but I could hear a man's voice drone over the marine radio. The voice methodically called out locations around the Bay and the associated times for high and low tides. I rolled over to look at Shenan, imagining I would find her asleep. To my surprise, she was awake, already looking up at me. She gazed at me with resolution.

"You're awake," I said over the slower drone of the engine.

"Jim, be honest with me," she said, sucking on a mint. "Where did you get this cushion?"

"From the boat I want to buy."

"How did you get it?"

"I borrowed it."

"Do they know you took it?"

"No."

"So, you stole it?"

"I borrowed it for a while. No one will even know it's gone."

"Did you hide it when you carried it away?"

I didn't answer. Shenan sat with her back against the wall and pulled her knees to her chest. "Do you want one?" she asked, tapping a tin of mints beside her. She didn't hand the mints to me, so I stepped down from my rack in nothing but my underwear. Sitting on the bench near her feet, I opened the tin and popped one in my mouth.

She took my hand. "I want to thank you for what you did last night."

"You already did."

"I know, but I want to do it sober."

"For the fishermen?"

"For everything. For carrying me away from the bar when I was being stupid. For stealing this cushion for me.

And yes, for protecting me from those fishermen. No one has ever thrown a man off a boat for me." She chuckled.

I wanted to tell her that I nearly threw two guys out of the shower room as well, but she didn't need to know that. "It was nothing."

"Can you believe what he said?"

"Who?"

"The one who asked whether you had had your way with me."

"That's just the way men talk around here."

"That's the way men talk everywhere."

"You're probably right, but I—"

"Jim.".

"Yes?"

She took my hand and placed it on her waist, then placed her other hand on my chest. "Just shut up and kiss me."

Her breath tasted like peppermint with a hint of alcohol. One of her legs rose against my body. I put my hand behind her neck and kissed down toward her chest again. With her lips just above my good ear I heard her sigh. We were interrupted then by another change in the drone of the engine. Joe had reined the throttle to an idle. I backed off slightly, waiting to see if Joe would open the hatch. He rapped on the door, the signal that he needed me to lower the anchor.

"I'll be right there," I yelled. Shenan slowly let go of me and hugged her knees as if they were my replacement. She rested her cheek on one knee. "I wish we'd woken up an hour ago," she said.

I slipped my clothes and boots on but stopped when I put my hand on the doorknob. "Maybe we should go ashore when we get a chance."

"Maybe we should."


After anchoring, Joe informed us that the Department of Fish and Game had opened a six-hour window from eight in the morning to two in the afternoon. He had already talked to Phillip via the radio. Apparently, the *Nereid's* engine was back together, but Steve had quit.

"Why?" I asked.

"I don't know." I wondered if it had something to do with my note. Joe turned to Shenan. "Your uncle said he needs you to fish with him."

"Really?" She looked at me with a shocked expression, then returned her attention to Joe. When?"

"When he gets over to this side. Maybe tonight. Maybe tomorrow."

"Okay." She turned to me again.

I shrugged. "The bright side is that we'll still tie up together."

"You're right. It's not like it's goodbye." As we fished, we determined not to talk about her leaving the boat. Instead, we talked about caribou and college, and oil and biology. But the day hinged on news we heard over the marine radio during our lunch break.

"In case anyone's interested," an unknown voice said over the common channel, "there's a whale carcass north of Cape Menshikof. Stevenson said he saw some wolves on it. They spooked when he went by."

Shenan looked at me like she had seen a ghost. "Where's Cape Menshikof?"

I turned to Joe for the answer. "Far away," he said. "We would have to leave soon, after going to the tender."

"How far?"

"Maybe fifty miles."

"I see."

"We wouldn't get there until late evening."

She nodded her head, though it was obvious she wanted to say more.

"We can go," Joe said, "but you probably won't see them."

"We can go?"

"If you want to. We will miss only an hour of fishing."

It seemed like a long shot to me. Who knew if we could find the whale carcass on that long, lonely stretch of beach, let alone see wolves on it, but it was worth a try. "I'm game."

Joe got on the radio to pinpoint the location but learned little more. We hailed Phillip on a side channel and shared our plans. He would head that way, he said. We found the closest tender ship, unloaded a decent catch of fish, and headed south as fast as the *Mikilak* could go.


All afternoon, and into the early evening, we motored toward the Bering Sea. We passed old canneries and an occasional boat, but it was clear that we passed farther and farther from civilization. Joe slowed to an idle when we came across two humpback whales feeding ravenously in the water. Their flukes and tails waved forcefully in the air. Shenan took pictures. I knew that this sight alone made the trip worth it, so I worried less about finding the whale carcass at the end of the quest.

Around eight o'clock we passed Ugashik Bay where the small village of Pilot Point lies. On the radio, we were told that we would find the carcass five to ten miles south of this spot. Joe got out his binoculars and glassed the beach from a safe distance from the sand bars near the shore. While we searched, I asked if Shenan and I could take sleeping bags with us to spend the night ashore.

After a minute in which I wasn't sure that he would answer, he said, "That's fine. You can take the flare gun."

"In case we get lost, or for the wolves?"

He shrugged as he peered through the binoculars, then handed them to me and pointed. "There," he said.

"I see it." A massive black mound lay on the beach just below the green grass which led to a spine of low hills in the distance. It didn't look like something that had been alive, but the prominent ridges on what must have been its belly showed it to be a whale. I didn't see any wolves. I handed the binoculars to Shenan who scoped the shore for a long time before handing the binoculars back to Joe.

"I don't see any wolves," she said.

"I saw one. He's probably on the back side now." Joe throttled down to an idle. "If we go closer, we will spook him."

"What should we do?" I asked.

"Do you want to go ashore?"

"Yes."

"I will take you back to the inlet by the bay. You can jump from there. Then, you hike."

"Perfect," I said, glancing at Shenan. She clasped her hands in front of her mouth like she was praying.

"Be careful. Respect the wolves." Joe looked down at the console. His finger ran down the tide table near the wheel. "Meet me at the inlet at 6:20 a.m."


Joe steamed back toward the inlet while Shenan and I packed our bags. "This is so exciting," she kept saying. Shenan had changed into jeans and a tight sweater with horizontal stripes. I grabbed my sleeping bag and an extra blanket and stuffed them in my backpack. I didn't exactly know what we planned to do. Vague notions of sex filled my mind, but I was not thinking about specifics. My heart raced. I threw the pack over my shoulder and went to the cabin.

Joe handed me the flare gun. "I will be anchored near Ugashik."

"Thank you," I said, stuffing the orange gun into my pack.

"Thank you, Joe," Shenan said, giving him a kiss on the cheek. "We're tired of being cooped up on the boat."

Joe could have mentioned that we had been on the boat for only twenty-four hours, but he only nodded.

Though it was night, the sun had not set below the horizon. The *Mikilak* weaved into a small creek surrounded by steep black mud. Beyond that lay an endless ocean of grass. Joe eased the boat toward the bank.

I turned to see if Shenan was ready to jump. I found her facing the weak sun, basking in its light even if it gave no heat. She opened her eyes and looked at me. Indescribable agitation filled my body. I don't think Shenan sensed what I knew—that this was dangerous.

"You realize we have to jump ashore in a few seconds, right?"

She scrambled to her feet and followed me to the bow. The edge of the bow made a sloughing sound as it edged onto the silt. I took a few steps and jumped. Shenan landed a few feet behind me. Safely on dry land, we turned and waved at Joe who already had the boat in reverse. "Be careful!" he yelled.

"We will," we yelled in unison.

Turning toward me, she asked, "Where do we go?"

"That way," I said, pointing. She strode over the tidal mud into the twilight, her jeans swaying beneath her small backpack. Her ribs narrowed like a "V" down to her waist, pointing me in directions I had never been but seemed to understand so well. I no longer thought about the future. I no longer debated our compatibility. I listened to the directions imprinted deep within my soul, a language I did not fully know until Shenan's body decoded it for me. Her body had been speaking to me in that language all summer—the pitch of her voice, the accidental smile, the sway of her hips. I heard it and followed.

Reaching the marsh grass, she stopped and glanced at me over her shoulder. My body bumped up behind her as I placed my hands on her hips. She craned her neck back and kissed me. Then she looked ahead and scanned the area like an animal searching for prey. In the fading light, I saw nothing but waves of grass blowing in the wind. No brush or trees, just small hills, a flat plain, the beach, and the endless bay.

"Let's find the whale," she said.

"Follow me." I took the lead, walking quickly. The water, now, was nothing but a dark gray space off to our right. After forty-five minutes, we reached the back side of the hills that I believed would shield our approach to the whale carcass. "Okay," I said as quietly as possible. There was a stiff offshore breeze blowing loudly in our ears, masking the sound of our movements. "Let's go a little farther down this side." I held my finger to my mouth then motioned for her to follow.

Passing along the backside of the hills, we came across a small wooden boat, a dory, a remnant of the early days when men fished with homemade nets in small double-enders like this one. It was beamy—about thirty feet long and more than ten across. It looked like a mirage, an unmanned vessel blowing listlessly over a sea of grass, waiting for someone to take the helm, waiting to take us on a journey. Some nights I fancy that it appeared only for us and disappeared the next morning, floating away into the sea and over the horizon. We went to examine it more closely. Weeds and grass grew through cracks in the hull, but it still had a smooth plankboard floor. It had been white once. Running my hand along the floorboards, I said quietly, "This is perfect. The gunnels will shield us from the wind and the floor will keep us off the ground. Do you want to sleep here tonight?"

"That sounds delicious," she said, looking more at me than at the dory.

"Let's leave our packs here. I think the whale is on the other side of the hill."

Shenan nodded enthusiastically. As I removed the orange flare gun from my pack and stuffed its barrel into my back pocket, Shenan held her hand to her mouth and tried to suppress a few coughs. They came out muffled, but I knew the breeze would carry the sound away from the beach and not toward it.

"This is crazy," I whispered, but could tell that I was smiling from ear to ear.

She nodded, wide-eyed. "This is already the best night of my life and it hasn't even started."

"Okay, here's the plan. We're going to crawl to the top of the hill and lay low." I made crawling motions with my hands. "Stay close to me. We probably won't see anything, but if we do, we have to stay together."

"Okay."

"And whatever you do, don't run."

"Okay."

"Ready?"

"Yes."

Hunched over, I hiked up the grassy slope which separated us from the beach. Imitating me, she followed. Nearing the top, we got down on our bellies and crawled with our elbows in the tall grass. A sobering thought struck me—the carcass could attract bears as well. My pulse quickened. I debated telling Shenan but knew that it wouldn't change our actions.

Nearing the top, my heart pumped like it might explode. Checking one last time to make sure she was right beside me and the flare gun was in my pocket, I slowly stuck my head up over the crest of the hill. The breeze, which blew hard over the hilltop, hit me with a stench of decay that made me catch my breath. But it was worth it. The giant black body of the whale lay fifty yards down the hill on the beach. I exhaled deeply when I saw no bears.

The dim light from the horizon came from behind the big black body. I glanced at Shenan to see if she saw anything. "Do you see them, Jim?" she whispered. "Do you see them?"

I returned my attention to the carcass and peered as deeply as I could. Once my eyes adjusted, I saw a lighter gray body moving near the bottom of the black hulk. "I see it," I whispered.

"There's two," she said. The foul breeze blew so loud in my ears that I could barely hear her.

"Oh my gosh, you're right." Peering carefully, I saw the second one lounging in the dark sand apparently satiated from a long day of feasting.

"I have to get my camera," Shenan said. She backed down the hill on her elbows. My attention returned to the first wolf. He, or she, tugged at some of the whale's tissue near the head. As I watched, a third wolf, a very dark one, climbed on top of the whale from the far side. He appeared like a silhouette in front of the faint glimmering ocean behind him. He stopped on top of the whale, his head pointing in our direction. Though I couldn't make out his face, I imagined him looking straight at me. One wolf was an interesting sight. A second wolf was a bonus. But the sight of a third wolf changed my feelings in significant ways. It made me feel outnumbered.

I turned to see where Shenan had disappeared to. What I found stunned me. Shenan stood on top of the grassy hill twenty yards to my right watching the wolves as the wind fanned her hair behind her. She was naked. *She* was the object that attracted the third wolf's attention. The sight paralyzed me. I gawked at her, petrified by equal parts shock and wonder. I felt that if I moved or said anything, she would run toward the wolves like a wild animal.

I was right.

I called her name. She ignored me or didn't hear me. Instead, she started slowly down the hill.

"Shenan, what the hell are you doing?"

I crawled toward her, repeating my question.

She stopped briefly and turned to me. In a clear voice, she said, "Jim, I'm going to need my inhaler." Then she turned toward the wolves and started to jog.

I wanted to cuss at her for the dilemma she created for me. I was equally troubled by her proximity to the wolves and her propensity toward asthma attacks. I ran to the dory and her things, fully intending to return to her immediately and tackle her to the ground. I reached her pile of clothes, swearing under my breath. "I just told you we had to stick together!" I found myself saying. Nothing was in her pants pockets. "So help me God if you start running!" I searched recklessly through her bag, spewing its contents onto the ground. I turned to look for her, but she was gone over the spine of the hill. I found her inhaler, then grabbed the blanket out of my pack and ran to find her.

Breathlessly cresting the hill, I found something I will never forget. Shenan was indeed running—and so were the wolves. The three animals had scattered from the carcass and were now loping complacently along the grassy plain between the hills and the beach. Shenan ran parallel to them and slightly behind them, separated by fifty yards. All four animals were already several hundred yards from me. I bolted in that direction as fast as I could in my heavy boots. Shenan ran faster as the wolves fled farther from her. Everything was a gray blur except for her naked body, which stood out among the muted colors. Burdened by my boots and the blanket in my arms, I gained on her slowly.

After a minute of running, I saw her slow, then stop, then fall to her hands and knees. I caught up to her and found her coughing. Hunched over, the bumps of her spine stood out like the line of hills next to us. She looked frail in her nakedness while she coughed profusely. A few glances ahead and behind told me that the wolves had fled out of sight.

"I have your inhaler!" Placing one hand on her back, I handed the inhaler to her with the other. Her skin was ice cold. Quickly unfolding the blanket, I draped it over her and held it closed around her stomach.

"I swear to God, Shenan, once you recover, I'm going to kill you." She spit phlegm on the ground and caught a moment to breathe deeply from her inhaler.

What must have been only a few minutes dragged on interminably while she coughed and tried to regain her breath. Finally, still hunched over, she spoke. "Did you see that, Jim?"

"Yes, I saw it."

"Wasn't it beautiful?"

"I think terrifying is the word."

"Did I worry you?"

"Yes, and I'm still worried. Are you okay?"

"This happens all the time." She coughed more. "Thank you for my inhaler."

"You did that on purpose."

"Maybe."

I rubbed the wool blanket back and forth over her skin trying to generate friction. "As soon as you can, we need to get you back to your clothes. If the wolves or the asthma don't kill you, the cold will."

She stood slowly, breathing deeply, coughing intermittently. She smiled at me with the blanket falling from one shoulder. "And if none of those things kill me, you're going to, right?"

"I haven't decided yet," I said, warmed by the sight of her looking healthier. I pulled the blanket onto her bare shoulder and wrapped it tight around her neck. "I would carry you, but walking will probably warm you more."

"But I want to feel your warmth."

I picked her up and began the long walk to the dory and our things. Along the way, her breathing returned to normal. I looked behind us sporadically, but the wolves never returned. Shenan talked animatedly about her adventure. She recalled every moment, the way each wolf looked at her, how she "had a moment" with the dark one, and how her wildest dream had just come true.

When we came to the dory and our things, I placed her feet on the ground. By this time, she looked like a perfectly healthy person again, and I wondered if my mind had exaggerated the coughing due to runaway fear. Down in the small valley, there was no breeze, and the smell of decay did not reach the boat. Still wrapped in the blanket, she stepped into the dinghy and onto the floorboards.

"Are you coming in?" Her hand reached for me from the folds of the blanket. I took it and stepped into the little boat. She kissed me. I slipped my hands into the blanket, resting them on her naked hips. Her skin had warmed considerably, but her hands and cheeks were cold. She unbuttoned some of my shirt and placed her hands on my ribs, which made me flinch. She seemed to like that and made a game of putting her cold hands everywhere before finishing the buttons on my shirt. The blanket fell from her body. "You're going to freeze to death," I said, removing my shirt.

"Not with you on me."

"Let me get the sleeping bag."

"No." She pulled me down onto the blanket. I kissed her—on her face, neck and shoulders. Rising again to my knees, I unbuckled my belt. She raised herself up on one arm and placed her other hand on mine. "Jim?"

"Yes?"

"Am I making you do things you don't want to do, things that you'll regret?"

I thought a moment, knowing exactly why she would ask me that. Then I looked at her sitting naked on a blanket, her face tender and concerned. Seeing her there, her long hair covering her breasts, her eyes sparkling in the moonlight, I felt closer to heaven than I ever had. I worshipped her, an earthly thing, and for that alone I am sorry. I looked at the swaying grass for just a moment and I knew what to say. "The only thing I would regret is not doing this." She smiled and helped me with the buckle. Standing, I quickly removed my jeans and boots.

She giggled when I finished. "What about your socks?" she asked.

"They'll keep me warm."

She raised herself on her arms again and glanced toward her pile of clothes. "Perhaps I should put mine on, too." It was her first admission that she might be cold.

I retrieved her long colorful socks from the pile. As I right sided them, she extended a foot toward me. She watched me put her socks on. "Does that feel better?"

"I'm still freezing. Get over here." I knelt over her and she pulled her hair away from her breasts. I reached down and kissed them as she leaned back on her arms. She let her head fall backward until I kissed every inch of her chest. She laid down and pulled me over her. I kissed her neck and began to rock between her legs. She reached one hand up to the boat behind her. The other held tightly to the back of my neck. Her eyes peered straight into mine, and I saw every detail in them. Her pupils had grown so large in the twilight that the golden ring of each iris blazed like the corona of an eclipsed sun. Minutes passed. Sometimes she lay open-mouthed, her chest heaving, her eyes peering into the great ocean above. Sometimes she closed her eyes and turned to the side, gasping for air. But most of the time, her eyes looked straight into mine.

When it was over, I got the sleeping bag from my pack, and we climbed in. It shielded our skin from the rough wool blanket beneath us. The night was very cold, and we held each other tight. Shenan nestled the cold tip of her nose into the corner of my neck and shoulder. We slept in each other's arms, lying in a boat that drifted on an ocean of grass.

# Chapter 14

# An Unkindness of Ravens

Tonight, I heard a wolf howl. I opened the window of Finn's cabin to listen. When the wolf cried out again, I tried to pinpoint its provenance. I know that the Chekok Creek pack ranges this territory, but much of their activity remains inside the Lake Clark National Park to the north. Besides, no pack answered. It was a lone wolf. I felt certain it was the same black wolf I had seen several times near my home in Iliamna. She appears to be a yearling. Both she and one of her brothers left the Chekok Creek pack, most likely in the hopes of finding new families. There are several packs to the north, and some south of the lake. The last I heard from the wolf research team, the brother had taken up residence with a new pack a hundred miles south of here. Clearly, his sister had not. I had hopes that she would form a new pack with one of the males from the disbanded Kijik River pack, but they have gone west without her.

Several weeks ago, I saw her near my cabin. It was obvious then that she was hungry. Wolves are effective hunters in large groups. On their own, however, their hunting prowess diminishes greatly. Instead, they scrounge for small animals, as well as the dead and diseased. When I saw her hungry eyes, I instinctively wanted to help her. Of course, I left her alone.

While the sound brought me great joy, I couldn't help but wonder if it brought different emotions to some of the town's residents—possibly fear or anger. I made a mental note to remind the villagers to continue to avoid the wolf and to never feed it. If time allows, I might inspect the village's waste site. But it is far too late for that now. Leaving the window open, I return to my writing.

—

I awoke in the early morning twilight, lying with Shenan in the dory. There were very few clouds in the sky. It would be a bright day soon. Shenan lay beside me with her head on my backpack. I thought about the night before and my mind brimmed with exuberance. I felt that the rest of my life would be filled with nothing but wonderful things. I raised my head and glanced around, just to be sure we weren't in the company of wolves. I saw nothing but grass and sky and a lone mountain in the distance.

Shenan and I lay close together. There was little room in that one sleeping bag, and it had been a chilly few hours. One of her long, naked thighs rested over my own. Her upper body lay snuggled next to mine and her hand rested on my chest. Only our heads protruded from the sleeping bag. The sharp, chill air reddened her cheeks and nose. Her breaths wheezed in and out methodically.

I didn't wake her. I didn't want to move. I didn't want anything to change for the rest of my life. Unfortunately, I had to urinate badly. I looked at my watch—we had a little over an hour before our rendezvous with the *Mikilak*.

Everything felt surreal. Everything about the night before felt like a dream—the whale, the wolves, chasing Shenan in the moonlight, the sex.

The sun rose higher in the sky as I watched her sleep. New details of her face revealed themselves in each new angle of light. This was the first time I noticed how long her eyelashes were. They rested peacefully at the bottoms of her eyes. Occasionally she stirred, and slight grimaces appeared at the corners of her mouth. She looked so innocent, which was a sharp contrast to her fierce independence and fiery temper. It was hard to believe she was the same person that had already slapped me two or three times and shoved me into the ocean. I was slowly learning that there were three Shenans. In the morning she was happy, optimistic, and pure. During the day she was bound by earthly concerns, prone to anger, rebellion, and action. At night, she was a manic being possessed by spirits and whims, a dreamer, an adventurer, someone who wanted to be carried along and taken on a journey.

True to these characteristics, I predicted that she would wake up like an innocent child ready to start the process anew. I enjoyed puzzling over her personality, but we had to return to the boat. It was crucial that we met Joe at the precise time and, hopefully, that was before the fishing period opened. I woke her. Her eyes squinted in the weak sunlight, then adjusted, opening to something less than their full radiance. She looked around for a second then turned to me, giving me a weak smile.

"We have to meet Joe in an hour. Plus, I have to pee really bad."

She giggled, which turned into a cough. Under the sleeping bag, she embraced me with one arm and kissed my shoulder. "Okay," she said. She unzipped the sleeping bag, sat up and stretched like a mermaid on a rock. I was immediately and unexpectedly aroused. I sat up and kissed the top of her bare sternum. She put her hands in my hair and giggled. "Do you think they came back?" she asked.

"I don't know, but I'll check." I let go of her reluctantly, put on my pants and boots, and peed a few paces away. Repeating my actions of the previous night, I climbed the hill and slowly peered over the crest. The breeze was not as strong, but it still smelled of carrion. Now fully illuminated, the features of the whale manifested in sharp detail. There were no wolves. A host of ravens plucked at white decaying flesh where it lay open in the otherwise black hulk. I had heard that when ravens find a dead animal, they call wolves to the location to open it up for them. I wondered if these ravens had called the wolves here.

I retraced my steps down the hill, not worrying about secrecy, but turned away when I found Shenan peeing in the grass on the other side of the dory. I told her what I saw.

"You can look now." She stood up now and returned to the boat wearing only her underwear and sweater. "I guess it was too much to hope for—seeing them again."

"Probably."

"It was better than anything I ever dreamed of."

"I'm surprised that a city-girl like you got so used to peeing in the open."

"I may be a city-girl, but I'm no modernista."

"A what?" I asked, rolling the sleeping bag.

"It's a word I made up. My Spanish teacher always said I'm an optimista, and somehow I changed the word with my friends." She buttoned her jeans, then zipped them. "It means someone who's out of touch with the past—someone who doesn't know where we came from. For most of human history, everyone had to pee in the bushes." She gathered her boots and sat on the gunnel of the dory, rubbing her foot.

"Only a woman can be that insightful."

"You know what I like about you, Jim? I love the way you talk about women."

"That's good. I thought you might be keeping me around just to be an Alaska guide."

"And that, too," she said, laughing, then started to cough. "I'm going to be awhile," she said. She walked around to the other side of the dory, even though it afforded little privacy. Laying a hand on the gunnel of the boat, she bent over and coughed profusely. I heard her spit.

"Shenan," I said, returning the sleeping bag to my pack, "you have tuberculosis or something."

"Can you pound on my back?"

I went to her, still bent over with her hands on her knees, and pounded on her back with one palm.

"Both hands, and faster."

I beat rapidly with both fists, moving up and down her back.

"Good," she said. She continued to cough and spit. After a few minutes, the fit abated. "Sexy, isn't it."

"I don't mind."

"You can stop now." She stood and took a deep breath, followed by a few shots of her inhaler. She went to her backpack. "Jim, there's something I need to tell you."

"Good. Because I was just about to ask a lot of questions."

"Let's walk and talk."

We started at a brisk pace. The night before, we had stayed on the inland side of the spine of hills, which had blocked our view of the sea. This time, we crossed over the crest of hills and for the first time that morning Shenan saw the whale carcass with its host of ravens.

"Wow, there must be a hundred of them," she said. "Wait here." And for the second time in less than a day, Shenan went running toward the dead whale and the animals that gorged themselves on it. It soon became apparent what her intentions were. Reaching the tidal mud, she spread her arms and ran at the flock. The black scavengers exploded into a dark cloud above the carcass, but rather than dispersing, they turned and watched from the air as she dipped her arms left and right like she was flying around the whale. After a minute of playing with the ravens, she hiked back to me. "That was fun," she said, wiping the sweat from her brow. The ravens returned and resumed their feasting.

I reached for her hand and laughed. "Are you done now?"

"You should have joined me."

"I should have, but we need to get back to the boat."

We continued north toward Pilot Point with the vast bay stretching all the way to the horizon on our left. Many miles ahead of us, snowy Mount Peulik rose toward the sky. There was nothing around us except blue ocean, gray beach, green grass, and a white mountain.

We walked hand in hand. I imagined it was some sight, the two of us stepping proudly over the hills, the wind blowing through our hair. But we were at the far edge of the earth and no one witnessed us but the ravens who occasionally circled overhead. We hiked for a minute before she started talking.

"First of all, I have to ask you something."

"Okay."

"You don't have any regrets, do you?"

"About last night or about not running toward the ravens?"

She laughed. "About last night."

"None."

"Okay, good."

"Why do you ask?"

"I know you're very religious."

"I haven't thought about that part much."

"Okay, I hope it doesn't change anything."

"Now, can I ask you a question?"

"Of course."

"Why are you so sick and not getting better?"

Shenan cast her eyes at the ground in front of us. "I haven't told you this because . . . Well, I needed time and space to *not* think about it this summer. That was very important to me." She stopped and turned to me. She took both my hands. "Jim, I don't have asthma. I have a disease called cystic fibrosis."

"What's that?"

"It's a disease I was born with. It causes the mucous and fluids in my body to be thick. That's why my lungs are always full and why I have to cough so much. I get infections a lot, so I take antibiotics every day. It's also why my sweat is so salty."

We started walking again.

"Is there a cure?"

"No. And here's the worst part. I've been told that I won't live past my twenties."

My stomach flipped. "Past your twenties?"

She bit her lip. "In fact, most people with CF don't make it to their twenties."

I had nothing to say.

"Let's keep walking or we'll be late," she said. I hadn't realized we'd stopped again. Shock and anger diffused through my body as I started haphazardly toward the boat.

"Do you have any questions?"

"A lot of questions, but don't really know what they are. Does your uncle know?"

"Yes. He's known since I was a little girl."

"Joe?"

"Sometimes I think he does. My uncle might have told him."

"Are you . . . I don't know how to say this. Are you very sad?"

"I'm both sad and angry at times, but I've had a long time to come to grips with it. I've known I didn't have much time since I was ten years old."

"Your parents told you?"

"Yes."

"That's a lot for someone to digest."

"What is?"

"To know that you have a terminal illness."

"Not really. Jim, don't you realize that you're just like me and every human who has ever lived. We all have a terminal illness."

A blast of empty space struck me, leaving an open hole in my chest. It grew outward until the nothingness consumed my entire being.

"You see, I feel fortunate because I know about the limitations of time better than most people."

"Is that why you came to Alaska?"

"Yes, that's exactly why. I'm trying to live as much life as I can—fast and slow at the same time. Seeing the wilderness was one of my dreams. Seeing wolves was one of my dreams. I never thought it would come true. And it did, because of you. And Joe, of course. And the universe helping me, I think."

A thought struck me. "What other dreams do you have?"

"I don't have many specific ones, I guess. I truly feel fulfilled after last night . . . for many things that happened last night." She glanced at me with a wry smile. "I would like to see the caribou herds you described. But, of course, I had dreams, long-term dreams, but I gave up on them a long time ago."

"What dreams?"

"You know, the usual stuff. Getting married. Having a family. Homesteading. Those kinds of things."

"Maybe they'll still come true."

She shrugged her shoulders. "Maybe. I never thought I would go running with wolves, and that came true. I guess anything's possible."

She was an optimista. "If you can do that, who knows what else is in store."

Rising to the top of a small elevation, I spotted the small cove ahead of us, and saw the *Mikilak* just entering the inlet. The boat would be at the bank in a few minutes. To my surprise, another boat, the *Nereid,* lay anchored offshore. Shenan paused briefly when she saw her uncle's boat, then caught up with me again as we marched toward the cove.

Reaching the high muddy bank, Joe came out and cast a line to me before returning to the controls. "Let me do it," Shenan said. I handed her the line. She leaned back and pulled the boat closer to the edge. I got behind her to pull. "I can do it myself."

I stepped back and watched her pull the bow just to the edge of the silty shore. We climbed aboard as Joe switched the transmission into reverse.

"Did you see them?" Joe asked when we entered the pilot house.

"Yes, three of them," Shenan said. "It was beautiful and wonderful and the most amazing thing I have ever seen." Shenan described how we snuck up to the whale, and the appearance of the wolves. She failed to mention stripping off her clothes and running after them. "And then, after fifteen minutes or so, they ran away," she said, "and we never saw them again."

We motored out to the *Nereid* and tied onto her. Phillip looked at Shenan. "Where have you been?"

"We stayed ashore last night. We slept inside an abandoned boat."

"You failed to mention you went looking for wolves," he said. "Your parents would kill me if they knew about this."

"But I'm safe and sound, aren't I?"

He grunted. I saw then that the overly protective man I thought I knew had actually been giving her a long leash all summer. "I've been waiting for you."

"What for?"

"Steve quit, and there's still two weeks of fishing left. I need you to be my puller."

"But what about Joe's arm?"

"He said they'll get by. And I can't fish alone."

"I understand."

"It turns out the *Nereid* has a blown head gasket. I ordered a new one from Anchorage but can't replace it till the new one arrives on the next plane."

"Then how did you get here?" Shenan asked.

"She runs good enough for now. There's still plenty of time to keep the season from being a total bust, but we need to get farther east. The fishing window opens in an hour."

Shenan looked at me before she turned back to Phillip. "When are we leaving?"

"Now." He paused a moment. "Don't worry. We'll stick close to the *Mikilak*. I'm not chancing anything until I get a new gasket." He put his hand on her shoulder. "Sorry about this, Shenan, but we've got to go. Joe and I have already discussed it. Get your things."

I helped Shenan get her things while Joe and Phillip talked about where we would fish. If Shenan looked dejected, I must have appeared dazed. I felt like I had just been thrown over a waterfall, and I didn't know what lay at the bottom. I wanted to stay near Shenan. Strangely, I felt I should comfort her about her disease, but reminded myself that it was only news to me. She had been dealing with it her entire life.

I stepped down the few steps leading to the berthing compartment and rested my hands on the hatch above me. "What else can I carry?"

The corners of her eyes drooped when she looked at me. "Jim, I feel like you probably have so many questions. Or, maybe you don't. Or, maybe it doesn't affect you too much." Her eyes grew moist. She bit her lip.

I pulled her close and held her. "It affects me more than you know."

"That means a lot to me," she said, holding me tight. "I would love to talk more, but I have to get my things." She backed away and reached for her copy of *Never Cry Wolf* lying on her cushion. "Do you remember when we drew these things by the pond?" She opened the front cover and showed me the sketches we'd drawn of the log cabin and the river. "I want you to have this, and no matter what happens I want you to make these dreams come true. And there's something else." She turned to the back cover where she had written her name, address and phone number in Virginia. She handed it to me. "I know I'm not leaving and I'm probably going to see you tonight and for several more weeks, but I want you to have this."

I tried to be light-hearted. "Thank you, but why read about running with the wolves when I've already done it for real?"

She chuckled.

Joe came into the pilot house above us. "How's it coming?"

"I think I've got it all," she said. "Jim, can you get my guitar?"

She picked up her backpack and sleeping bag. I grabbed the hard guitar case. Joe said he needed to pay her.

"Oh, I know you're good for it, Joe. We can do that tonight or some other day."

"Ok." He moved away from the doorway to make room for us.

Shenan stopped in the doorway, her sleeping bag squeezed tightly between us. She looked me in the eyes and smiled. "Thank you for everything, Jim," she said.

"Everything so far, you mean."

"You're right, for everything so far."

# Chapter 15

# Salmon Woman

I convened another public meeting today to discuss the killing of both the dentist and the illegal killing of the grizzly. It's safe to say that ninety percent of the town showed up.

"First things first," I told them, "the Department of Fish and Game is doing everything it can to protect the public from any dangerous bears."

I heard snickers in the crowd.

"And what might that be?" a man named Rich Gregson asked. He wore jeans, a flannel shirt and suspenders. His arms, resting on his bulging belly, lay hidden under his long beard.

"We have a plan—the one I outlined at the last meeting. The DNA analysis on the hair samples has been completed, and we're bringing a helicopter to tranquilize bears in the area. I have surveyed the area and have seen numerous bears along that stretch of the river. It could be any one of them. When the helicopter arrives, we're going to tranquilize several of those bears and take DNA samples. Those bears will also be collared. If the DNA matches the DNA taken from the body, that bear will be located again and euthanized."

"Why not kill all of the bears along that stretch of the river?" Gregson asked. "That could have been done by now."

"If we did that, where would we stop? After we've killed two bears? Ten?"

"As many as we need to. It's the summer. There are children in the village."

"Let me ask you a few questions, Mr. Gregson. Do you know how many people live in the Lake and Peninsula Borough?"

"A few thousand."

"Less than two thousand actually. And how many brown bears live in the borough—not including black bears?"

"You're the biologist."

"You're right—that's something you probably wouldn't know, but it's something you need to know. There are ten thousand brown bears in this Borough. We can't start shooting bears along the river. There would be no end to it. More importantly, we'd never know if we got the right one."

"Perhaps we already did get the right one," a man named Don Iffrig said. He sat near Gregson.

"Who's we?" I asked. "Who shot the bear, Mr. Iffrig?"

"I don't know."

I eyeballed him a second more to see if he would squirm. "I actually have an answer to that question, which was tonight's second topic. We don't have DNA results on the samples from the dead sow yet, but microscopic analysis of the hairs suggested they were from two different bears. The hairs found on the tourist's body were decidedly darker, while the dead sow is somewhat blonde. We'll know for certain when the DNA is analyzed, but for now it looks pretty certain that she had nothing to do with the tourist's death."

"What about the wolf?" Iffrig's wife, Nancy, asked. "Is Fish and Game doing anything about that?"

"The black wolf?"

"Yes."

"What about it?"

"That wolf is getting too bold. He was seen near the old school road a few days ago."

"Was it acting suspiciously?"

"No."

"Did people make noise to scare it away?"

"I don't think that it got close enough."

"Has anyone left any trash or meat out?"

"Not to my knowledge. But don't you think it could be dangerous?"

I repeated a mantra I have said over a hundred times in my life. "Wolves will not hurt people ninety-nine percent of the time."

"You don't think wolves are dangerous?" Nancy asked.

"That's not what I said. I said they will not hurt people ninety-nine percent of the time."

I feel like I've had this same conversation over and over for many decades. The most renowned version took place more than a decade ago when testifying before the state senate on aerial wolf hunts. Senator Kitchner questioned me. "Mr. LaBerg," she said, looking over the top of her glasses, "would you categorize wolves as bloodthirsty killers or mostly friendly animals?" "Neither," I said, "they are wolves." "Could you clarify that statement?" "Certainly. Wolves are animals that are very good at killing, but they will not harm humans in ninety-nine percent of encounters." "So, you think they're rather friendly?" "Not if you encounter them a hundred times." Some members of the crowd chuckled. "It seems to me, Mr. LaBerg, that you're rather evasive in your answers." "No, I think ninety-nine percent is quite specific. Of course, it's not a scientific number. And, truthfully, the scientific number is probably higher than ninety-nine. But I do know that one hundred percent of the time you should treat them as wild animals that *could* be dangerous." "Getting a straight answer from you is rather difficult." "Is it?" "Earlier, you said grizzly bears were safe ninety percent of the time." "Yes, they are far more dangerous." "It sounds like you would make every animal out to be potentially dangerous." "I think that sums up my thoughts fairly well." "If that's the case, what number would you apply to salmon?" she asked, which drew more chuckles from the crowd. "Well, I once saw a man get hit in the face by a jumping salmon. It knocked him down and gave him a black eye. So, I would say that salmon are safe ninety-nine-point-nine-nine percent of the time." This drew the greatest surge of laughs yet.

Today, I found myself in the same situation, trying to explain how dangerous wolves are. "In answer to your question, Mrs. Iffrig—no, the Department of Fish and Game is not doing anything about one wolf that has been traveling up and down the north side of the lake for two years without a single adverse event reported about her. Wolves get to live in this borough, too."

"Tell that to the family of the Chignik Lake teacher." Don Iffrig is a thin, wiry person, much like his wife.

"I fully appreciate your point, Mr. Iffrig. And that is exactly why I said wolves will not harm people ninety-nine percent of the time."

I am, of course, very familiar with the tragic event Iffrig alluded to. In 2010, a young woman from Pennsylvania was killed by wolves in Chignik Lake. She was a teacher in one of our many remote schools, none of which are accessible by road. One morning, the young teacher went jogging with headphones on and never returned. Her body was found partially consumed by animals and surrounded by wolf tracks. The state medical examiner determined the cause of death was "multiple injuries due to animal mauling." Eventually, eight wolves in the area were killed by the state. DNA found on her body matched the DNA of some of these animals. While we will never know exactly why she was attacked, it is quite clear that the woman was killed and partially eaten by wolves. None of them were rabid, and all but two were in good health. Chignik Lake is less than a hundred miles from where Shenan and I saw those wolves so many years ago.

It seemed ridiculous that Mrs. Iffrig would worry about a wolf in the middle of all these bears. The problem with most people, I thought, is that they don't understand numbers—senators included. "What's more important to keep in mind right now," I said, "is that brown bears are *far* more likely to attack humans than are wolves. And we know for a fact that there is a brown bear out there that has already killed one man. Everyone needs to be prudent and patient. Treat all wild animals as potentially dangerous. Have a plan. Tell people where you're going, and don't go into the wilderness alone. Stay in groups. With any amount of luck, we will identify the bear soon, and we will put him down before anyone else gets hurt. You always have the right of self-defense, but don't put yourself in a dangerous situation by taking matters into your own hands."

Gregson spoke up. "Why don't we do with the bears what Fish and Game did with the wolves in Chignik Lake? They killed six or eight wolves immediately after she was killed. They didn't wait to get the DNA results."

"There are many reasons, Mr. Gregson, but one of them is that only six to eight wolves lived in Chignik Lake. There are thousands of brown bears around here."

***

We fished hard the day Shenan returned to the *Nereid*—both boats did. When the Department of Fish and Game closed the fishing period, we delivered our catches to the tender and rendezvoused. I offered to cook for the four of us, which I did, but Shenan helped me around the tiny stove in the *Mikilak's* pilot house. We flirted and joked and laughed and talked about anything but cystic fibrosis.

And, of course, there was our hormones. And hormones are not an easy thing to deal with on two small boats tied together with other people on board. We kissed in the pilot house while the salmon baked. Soon, we were on top of the cushion where Shenan recently slept. Joe and Phillip talked in the stern of the *Nereid*. We did our best not to rock the boats.

The days ticked by like this—long periods of hard fishing, dinner at odd times dependent on government timing, intimate sessions snuck in whenever possible, and sleep, which was also dependent on the state biologists. Like most boats, we would fish as long as it was legal, even through the night. During one stretch that week, we fished for thirty hours straight with only light breaks for cat naps when we delivered our catch to the tender.

One night, Joe and I found that our path to the *Nereid* had been blocked by too many boats. Joe searched for a path, but an anchor line blocked the most promising route. "Sorry, Jim," he said. "We will just have to anchor here tonight. There's not much time for visiting anyway."

"I understand," I said. "It's probably God's way of getting us ready to say goodbye."

Joe frowned.

That night, after getting into our racks, he started to talk.

"Jim, did I ever tell you the story of Salmon Woman?" I could not see him, of course, as he slept in the bunk beneath mine. I opened my eyes. The little bit of sky that I could see through the portholes was gray with clouds. The boat bobbed gently. Little waves pattered hollowly against the hull.

"No."

"Raven was the leader of his people back in the early days of the earth. They lived near the ocean. He was a great chief, highly respected by his people, but his people were starving. They had no food. They wandered the forests looking for roots and berries and animals. But the animals had grown scarce, or they migrated off to other lands. Raven's people dug up all the roots around their village. They ate all the berries. Some ate the bark off the trees. They started to die.

"Raven had to do something. He had to find new food. They had paddled to the islands in search of roots and berries, but he wondered if there were more islands, farther than anyone had ever gone.

"Raven told his people that he was going on a journey to find food. He asked them to pray for him. He got into his finest canoe with only the clothes on his back, a cedar mat, and a hat made from a long piece of bark. He took only freshwater. Everyone knew that he might die.

"The people sang spiritual songs to guide him on his journey. He visited many islands but found nothing—only a few roots to keep him going. He was cold and starving. He canoed farther and farther. In his state of weakness, he began to sleep. He would wake up and paddle, then sleep some more. He grew weaker. He got lost. Fog set in. He didn't want to paddle in circles and was too weak to go on. He laid on the mat in his canoe and prayed to the Great Spirit. 'Great Spirit, I have failed my people. They are tired and starving, and they are relying on me to save them, but I cannot. I am not the leader I thought I was. I only wanted to save my people. I can feel it now—the Transformer is coming to take me to the spirit world.'

"He did not know that Salmon Woman was nearby. From the water, she listened to his prayer with deep compassion. She was impressed by his courage and his willingness to sacrifice for his people. She called on the Transformer to leave him alone and to come to her instead. She asked him to change her into a human.

"Raven lay in the canoe waiting for the Transformer. He heard loud splashing and the screams of a woman. He saw a woman struggling in the water. He paddled to her. With the strength he had left, he pulled her into the canoe.

"She was cold and wet. She wore a small dress made of otter fur. She lay on the floor of the canoe. It was Salmon Woman, who had transformed into a beautiful woman, but Raven did not know who she was.

"Raven gave her all that he had. He wrapped her body in the cedar mat and placed his hat on her head. He gave her the last water in his bag, then lay beside her to share his warmth. He thought that she would die.

"Then she spoke. 'You are a very great leader. I heard you pray. I have been watching you. I know what you are doing to save your people.'

"'Who are you?'

"'I am Salmon Woman. I have many children—more than you can imagine. They swim with me and follow me wherever I go.'

"'Where are they?'

"'They swim in the ocean. They are strong and healthy. Their skin sparkles like sunlight on rippling waters. They dance in the ocean where they eat until they are fat. They are obedient and come when I call.'

"'Where are they?'

"The young woman loosened the mat from her shoulders, sat up and removed the bark hat Raven had placed on her head. Sitting on her knees, she twirled her fingers in the water and began to sing. The clouds opened. She rose to her feet, stretched her arms toward the sky, the otter fur dripping water, her hair blowing in the wind. The auroras shone with the light of many moons. The waters around the canoe began to froth.

"'My children are here now,' she said, 'Let me show them to you.' She dipped the bark hat into the water and lifted a huge salmon. 'This is Chinook.' Again she dipped, and a smaller fish lay in the hat. 'This is Sockeye.' A third time she dipped. 'This is Coho.' A fourth and a fifth time she repeated the motions. 'This is Humpback. And this is Chum.' And a sixth time: 'This is Steelhead.'

"Raven had never seen children like this before, nor had he ever seen such a beautiful woman, nor heard such a beautiful song. 'Though my children are too numerous to count, I love them all. But I give my children to you. If your people are as generous as you, they surely deserve my children and your people will never starve again.'

"'I am grateful,' he said, 'but I am lost and do not know how to get back to my people.'

"'I will show you the way.'

"They found Raven's village by the river. They saw their leader return with a strange woman and strange meat. He told them his story and introduced Salmon Woman and her children. Raven's people soon learned how to cook good food from the meat.

"Raven knew only one way to repay Salmon Woman. He made her his wife. For many years, the people ate well because of her gift. But things changed.

The people grew tired of salmon. They ate salmon every meal. They smoked it and boiled it and fried it, and put it into cakes and soups. The people started to grumble. One day, when Raven was away on a hunting trip in the great forest, the people had had enough. 'I hate salmon,' someone said. 'I wish I didn't have to eat this,' said another. Salmon Woman heard them, and it broke her heart. She decided to take her children and leave the ungrateful people. She stepped out onto the beach, singing her song. She walked into the river and disappeared, taking her children with her.

"When Raven returned, he learned what had happened. He not only lost his wife, but he also lost the year-round supply of food that his people depended on. So, he went on a journey to find her. He did not know where she lived or how to get there. His only thought was to do what he had done before. He called for her, but she would not come. Just when he gave up hope, she appeared next to the canoe, and leaned on the gunnels. She still loved him, she said, and cared for his people, though they had greatly disrespected her children. He pleaded with her. She agreed to return to the village but said things would be different. From that point on, her children would only come during the spring and summer.

For the rest of the year, they would live in the ocean. That way, the people would not take her children for granted. Even Salmon Woman would not stay all year. Instead, she would be with her children in the ocean. Raven agreed to the terms. Salmon Woman climbed into the canoe and returned with him. From that day forward, the children of Salmon Woman came to the people every summer to provide all the food they needed. This is the time when the people started to pay great homage to Salmon Woman and her children. And from that day to this, the people have not been heard to grumble about eating salmon."

I stared at the overhead, fully entranced by the cadence of Joe's voice. I had never heard him tell a story before and didn't know why he had chosen to do so now. "That's beautiful, Joe."

Silence.

"What does it mean?"

There was no response from the bunk below. After a minute, I wondered if he had fallen asleep. Then, he said, "Those who don't appreciate what they have, don't deserve to have it."

My mind roused from the slumber into which it had fallen. I felt the entire thrust of the story had been directed at me. We spoke no more that night. Instead, my mind tossed and turned with questions and anxieties. Ideas popped into my head and took on a life of their own. Joe snored quietly in the bunk below me. I couldn't help but think that, somehow, he controlled my thoughts.

# Chapter 16

# **Dreams**

I had promised the villagers that the state was doing everything in its power to keep them safe. Apparently, that wasn't enough. After flying the hair and ballistic samples from the dead bear to Anchorage, I received bad news. Another attack occurred near Pedro Bay. A village man was mauled. He had severe wounds but had not been killed. The aerial medevac team from Anchorage whisked him away to one of the medical centers in the small metropolis.

Before he left, I visited him in the clinic. This is what I pieced together from talking to the victim and his friends.

The man had been fishing on the river, out of sight of his friends, when he was attacked. It was only one mile from the location where the dentist had been killed. Without warning, a bear seized him by the leg. His left thigh was flayed open with ribbons of flesh falling toward the knee. That is where the bear grabbed him and shook him before throwing him against a tree. The bear then rushed him again and bit off a large chunk of his right glute. He lay face down with his hands over his head while the bear took several more chunks out of his back and shoulders. His friends heard the commotion and came to the scene with a handgun. They shot at the bear twice before the animal charged away. They felt certain that at least one of the bullets hit the intended target.

I'm confident that this is the same bear, and now I have a description. He had a very peculiar color, the friend said, a blonde head that grew dark in front of his ears, with an almost black face. I knew this bear. He used to be quite big but was old now and had grown much thinner in recent years.

I found the man's blood-caked clothes in a plastic bag. Using medical gloves and tweezers, I teased through the folds until I found a few stray pieces of brown fur. I repackaged them in a forensic bag and sent them with the medevac aircraft. One of my colleagues in Anchorage would ensure they got to the lab.

After seeing the injured man off, the crowd of people who had gathered at the small airstrip turned their attention to me.

"I told you this would happen," Mr. Gregson said.

Nancy Iffrig poked me in the chest. "This is the state's fault."

"If we had just shot all the bears on that part of the river, this wouldn't have happened," her husband said.

I kept my responses as general as possible. "It's not certain whether we would have found the right bear." "The state is doing all that it can." "The bear will be euthanized soon."

"I'm holding you responsible," Mr. Gregson said, at least having the decency to carry some of my bags.

"I am responsible, Rich" I said, slinging my forensic bag over my shoulder, "and now I have the information I need to go after the bear."

"You're not waiting for the tranquilizing team?"

"No, but I'll need another trooper."

"What about the plan—the DNA results and radio collars?"

"I don't need them. I have a description now—of this bear, at least. And it's almost certainly the same bear."

"What does it look like?"

"It's a light-colored bear with a black face. Have you seen any bears like that?"

"No."

"That's good."

"We've seen the wolf, though."

"Just one?"

"Seems like it."

"Anyone see it near town?"

"I don't think so."

"Anyone head upriver since the incident?"

"No."

"Good. Let's keep it that way. There's a very dangerous animal out there."

\*\*\*

The day after Joe told me the story of Salmon Woman, we fished near the *Nereid*. I occasionally caught glimpses of Shenan and Phillip working hard. It was a profound juxtaposition to the beginning of the season when Shenan merely sat and watched the others. I knew from recent experience that Phillip would be deeply impressed by her work ethic. Likely, he had a hard time keeping up.

Around noon, Phillip hailed us with a wave of his arm, and we motored close. "Just got word on the radio," he said. "The new head gasket arrived. Gonna head to town while there's plenty of light, but we'll catch up to you guys in a few days."

I looked at Shenan who shrugged her shoulders. "Does Shenan need to go with you?" I asked.

Phillip laughed. "Sorry, Jim, but it's very hard to handle this boat by myself. And I'm not gonna kill myself trying to retrieve you guys from Cape Menshikof again. Besides, I might need help with the engine."

I nodded reluctantly, then pictured Shenan working on the engine, covered in grease. She had certainly left the role of housekeeper far behind. "Make sure you let us know when you get there."

"Will do!"

The *Nereid* pulled away from us as she rolled up and over a swell.

I waved at Shenan. The wind blew strands of dark hair across her face, just as it had five weeks before. She pulled her hair behind an ear, waved briefly, and forced a smile. I smiled as best I could.

When the fishing window closed that evening, and we had delivered our catch to the tender, I sat on the boat feeling bored. Phillip had reported over the radio that he and Shenan arrived safely in Dillingham. Joe said there would be no fishing the next day. Using their crude methods of counting fish, Fish and Game had determined what everyone already knew—too few fish had returned to the Bay that year.

We sat at anchor, and a vast loneliness settled over the water. She was gone, and with her, something disappeared from my world. I wanted to talk to her but couldn't. I could only think about her, and every time I thought about her, an impending sense of doom—like I was running out of time—flooded my mind.

Yet, the evening of Shenan's departure I found reprieve in the last thing she had given me—*Never Cry Wolf.* The book lay on a shelf near the bench she slept on. And for one brief minute, there was Shenan waiting to talk.

I picked it up and read. I enjoyed the author's sarcasm and wondered about his conclusion that wolves ate primarily mice and diseased caribou. By the second day of inactivity, my heart burned when I read about running naked with the wolves. It was like being with her again. What's more, as I read about the small wolf family, I grew to see Shenan in the author's description of the alpha female of the pack:

*"A slim, almost pure-white wolf with a thick ruff around her face, and wide-spaced, slightly slanted eyes, she seemed the picture of a minx. Beautiful, ebullient, passionate to a degree, and devilish when the mood was on her, she hardly looked like the epitome of motherhood; yet there could have been no better mother anywhere. I found myself calling her Angeline, although I have never been able to trace the origin of that name in the murky depths of my own subconscious. I respected and liked George very much, but I became deeply fond of Angeline, and still live in hopes that I can somewhere find a human female who embodies all her virtues."*

Laying the book aside, I determined that I had found the human Angeline. A dying Angeline. And who was I to her? A summer adventure? A last hurrah? What about all those dreams she had? What about my dreams? I opened the front cover of the book to look at the picture we had drawn several weeks before—a cabin and a farm on a river. And yes, just like the author with the wolf, I found unexpected joy in the thought of this charming, devilish creature being the mother of my children.

Before that summer, I didn't believe that a woman could be good yet mean, strong yet weak, motherly yet rebellious, submissive at times, but a supreme leader when need be, unapologetic for who she was, and not defined by another person. As I sat eating more peanut butter and jelly sandwiches well into the second day, I thought more about one of these notions in particular—the notion of a woman not being defined by a man. I thought about my mom as my father's wife, and my grandmothers as my grandfathers' wives. I recognized that many women looked for a man to define them. I am a doctor's wife, they say, or I am the wife of a farmer. Shenan was not like this. She was Shenandoah, a woman treading forward in life, not defined by society, but re-defining it. She seemed to pursue her passions without fear of mistake, exploring them for what they might teach her about life. Acutely intelligent, she made up her own mind about what to believe about the universe. She rushed headlong into the deep questions with confidence. She believed she had as good a chance as any to discover truth. Right now, and in every present moment, she was Shenandoah, a free spirit, one that no man could ever possess. But a man could experience life with her, and I wanted to be that man.

Three days later, we motored over to the Nushagak side of the Bay and met Shenan and Phillip near Clark's Point. We rafted up. Phillip was deeply frustrated by his discovery that he had ordered the wrong head gasket *after* he and Shenan had removed the cylinder head. He called Anchorage and ordered another. On the flip side, he couldn't believe his luck in not missing any fishing windows.

Shenan had something for me. Sitting in the *Mikilak's* pilot house, she handed me a box with a card. The card read: "Thank you for making my wildest dreams come true (and they are wild in every sense of the word)." That sentence ended with a smiley face. "I hope we have more adventures in the future."

I opened the box. It was an outfitters hat made of green felt, with a brown band and feather.

"I hope it fits," she said as I placed it on my head. It did.

"This is a good quality hat," I said, "a really practical piece of clothing."

"I don't think they sell a single thing in Dillingham that's not practical," she replied. "It's not exactly Fifth Avenue."

"That's true." I chuckled, then looked at my reflection in the glass. "I like it. I really do. I will keep it until it falls apart on my head."

"I'm glad."

"And I have something for you."

"Really?"

"Yes, but you have to wait till tonight to get it."

Before dinner, I got on the Marine radio and delivered a purposefully cryptic message: "Hey *Evelyn Marie, Tons of Fun*, and *Joanie Ray,* this is the *Mikilak.* Clark's Slough is looking good tonight." Several familiar voices came back with words like "ten-four" and "roger." If we had been in an open fishing window, boats would have flocked to Clark's Slough thinking I was signaling good friends to a fishing hot spot.

I told Shenan we were going on a date.

"Where are we going?"

"Ashore."

Shenan went below to change clothes then joined me on the deck. "We have to wait a bit," I said. It was late in the evening, so late that the northern sky faded into muted colors. The water lay low and reflective, becoming the same gray blue as the sky. Fingers of clouds stretched all the way to the horizon where they touched their own images in the water below. Around us, a fleet of lights glowed—a city of a hundred souls huddled in a place that was lifeless a few days before. The floating city sprang into being at night, and when the fishing windows opened, it disappeared like a fairy city evaporating. But on this night, like so many others, life flourished. Men played cards and drank spirits. Music drifted from a fishing boat in the distance. In this fairy city, the *Mikilak* and *Nereid* rested. A small dinghy motored toward us. It was Jan Gustavson bringing us his boat. He bumped up beside us, placing his hand on the gunnel. Grabbing a picnic basket hidden below the galley bench, I took Shenan's hand and motioned to the dinghy. Jan took her hand and helped her find a seat before switching spots with me. He climbed aboard the *Mikilak*, told us to have a good time, and joined Phillip and Joe aboard the *Nereid*. Shenan thanked him as I re-started the small outboard motor.

Gliding away, I watched Shenan sitting delicately in the bow. She wore her striped sweater, which was mostly covered by an unzipped rain jacket. Dark grease stains smeared the thighs of her jeans, scars from her crash course in engine mechanics.

"You've become quite an accomplished woman this summer."

"I like to think so. And I would have worn something nicer, but you told me to dress practically."

"Yes, that's good. And besides, I don't think there's anything you could wear that would make you look less beautiful."

She looked happy. She pulled her hair coquettishly behind one ear, smiled, and turned her attention forward.

By now, the sun had faded to twilight. Dark silhouettes perched on the edge of some boats, backlit by their cabin lights, their legs dangling over the water. They watched us as we motored by and raised luminous bottles in a gesture to our health and happiness.

"Where are we going?"

"You'll see. We're almost there."

I weaved through the boats, following a lane that led to the mouth of a small creek, a waterway much too small for anything other than a small dinghy. The creek lay in a deep, narrow gorge where a trail passed through a tangle of small alder bushes, a stark contrast to the nearly treeless terrain around us. Lanterns hung from the trees, looking like the fairy-town extended ashore, hidden in a miniature forest. Seeing all the lanterns, Shenan turned to me in wonder.

"I had a little help," I said.

I pulled the boat onto the muddy beach. Stepping onto the bank, my boots sank an inch into the mud. I carried the basket to the edge of the tidal zone and returned for Shenan. "Perhaps sneakers weren't a good idea," I said before picking her up and carrying her to solid ground. After grabbing the basket, I led the way into the narrow ravine, holding Shenan's hand. Many of the fishermen I knew had loaned their oil lanterns. Assorted shapes and sizes hung from the low trees, some of them old with glass bases and others modern with shiny metal. We passed slowly through the twisted branches, stepping over rocks and ducking under boughs. I thought briefly about bears and wondered if I should have brought the flare gun.

Halfway through the bramble, Shenan tugged at my hand, pulled me to her and kissed me passionately. She followed it with a foxy smile. The warmth of lantern-lights reflected in her warm, golden eyes.

We climbed a steep bank to a grassy knoll overlooking the slough and all the boats. Grabbing the last lantern, I spread a blanket on the ground just above the small glowing forest. We picnicked on crackers, cheese and a bottle of wine. She commented on the beauty of the night. We talked about her fishing accomplishments. We talked about how she was feeling and her daily struggles with cystic fibrosis. She seemed relieved to be able to talk candidly about struggling with pain and windedness. We ate and drank, watching the flow of the dark clouds in the dark sky. Then, feeling the time was right, I told her I had something I wanted to talk to her about.

I related my version of our short history together. I told her that I felt like the lucky man who had found the human Angeline. I told her that she had changed my life. I told her that I wanted to be the man who makes her dreams come true. I told her I wanted to be with her the rest of her life.

She stopped me. "Jim, are you sure about this?"

"I know it sounds crazy, but I'm sure."

"You know I don't have much time and that none of these dreams may ever come true."

"I know, but I want to try."

"I may become an invalid."

"Then you'll need someone to take care of you."

"What about college?"

"I'll quit. We can try for homestead land. I've decided I don't want to be a lawyer anyway. You did that. That's what I mean when I say you've changed me. You've helped me figure out my life."

"No. I won't let you quit."

"Why?"

"Because you want to be a biologist."

"Well, I can go back to school."

"If you quit, you won't go back. You'll get stuck fishing."

"That's okay. Like you said, it's the only way to make a living."

"But that is not your calling. You need to stay in school and study biology."

"Okay, but those are details."

"I know they seem like details to you," she said, "but I want to make sure you have a plan and that I'm not holding you back from that."

"I know what you're doing, but don't worry. What you just did—talking about what I should do—is exactly what I'm talking about. You know me so well that you know what I need more than I do. You can be nothing but a positive influence on my life. Being with you will put my life on track, not hold it back."

"Are you sure?"

"I've never been surer."

"We've known each other for less than six weeks."

"I realize that. I'm sure about this, but I'm starting to wonder if you don't feel the same way."

"Well I wouldn't jump to any conclusions," she said, looking happier. "No one has asked me anything yet."

I took her free hand in mine. "Shenandoah, will you marry me?"

She placed her hand on my cheek and looked deeply in my eyes. "Only if you're sure about this."

"I am."

"Then yes," she said slowly. "Definitely, yes." She kissed me, then touched her forehead to mine. "But this isn't just about my dreams. I want to make your dreams come true, too."

# Chapter 17

# Taking Flight

This morning, I went with Finn to the only restaurant in town for breakfast. Half the village was there. Some didn't even bother to eat—they just stood around and peppered me with questions while we ate.

"Are you going after the bear today?" Gregson asked.

"Probably not," I said, slicing the moose sausage. "I've requested backup. I'll give him one more day."

"What about the rally?" Finn asked.

"I'll do my best, Finn."

A young Native woman—maybe a teenager—asked, "Are you on social media?"

"Not much," I said, chewing the sausage.

"If you are, I wonder if you'd sign an online petition against the terrorists in the Southern Ocean."

A forkful of eggs paused in front of my mouth. "The terrorists in the Southern Ocean?"

"The ones who attack whale hunters."

"Oh, those ones."

"They're terrorists, you know."

"That's a bit harsh, don't you think?"

"Does that mean you're opposed to whale hunting?"

"I didn't say that."

"Whale hunting has been a part of my people's heritage for thousands of years."

"I understand that."

"So, will you sign the petition?"

"As a state official I can't get involved in things like that."

Of course, that was a lie. After all, I planned to voice my opinions on the Pebble Mine at a rally the very next evening. The young lady probably knew this and thought she could enlist me in her cause. More than anything, her passion about the Wilderness Warriors confused me, but I don't know why it should. The rift line between wilderness conservation and traditional Native lifestyles is the most complex issue I've had to balance throughout my career.

At least her questions had turned the conversation away from the failures of the state to protect the village—or, I should say, to allow the people to protect themselves. The very idea that it was the state's job to protect them was anathema to these people. They didn't want more action from the state. They wanted less. They were right to point out that the state's plan was complicated, and the fact that the helicopter had been delayed for a week due to bad weather only proved that. But laws are laws, and the state has a responsibility to preserve Alaska's wild creatures.

The discussion about the terrorists in the Southern Ocean only deflected attention for a minute. "So, now what?" Mrs. Iffrig asked. "Are you going to search from the air?"

"I already did," I said, pushing my empty plate away, reaching for my mug, "yesterday."

"I saw you flying around," the teenage girl said.

I finished my coffee. The waitress hovered over my shoulder with a fresh pot. I doubt she did it to provide excellent customer service. "More?" she asked.

"Just a little."

"Did you see him?" Mrs. Iffrig asked.

"I saw him."

"He was alive?"

"Yes. I saw him rummaging on the riverbank."

"Where?" Mr. Gregson asked.

"I'm not going to share that information just yet. It's a long hike from here. I'll get started first thing in the morning."

"Are you trying to protect a man-killer?"

"That's the opposite of what I'm trying to do. I'm going to kill the bear."

"Then why not tell us where he is?"

"Because killing him is my job. He is old and hungry. He has tasted human flesh and has learned that humans are easy targets. And, from what I've been told, he's also wounded. He's very dangerous. That's why I'm not telling anyone where he is."

"What if no backup arrives by tomorrow?"

"Then I'll just have to go alone."

"But you said everyone should stay in groups."

"I prefer to do this kind of thing with professionals. Loaded rifles behind me can be just as dangerous as the bears in front of me."

"I think we all know how to carry a gun," Gregson said.

"I know you do, Rich, but I also know people start acting weird around animals like this. Once an animal reaches mythic status, everyone wants to be the hero who slayed him."

"Do you have some sort of death wish or something?" Mr. Iffrig asked.

"No. I've already requested another wildlife agent. I don't know if he'll arrive tomorrow or the next day, but we can't wait longer. Whether he gets here in time or not, I'm heading out in the morning."

A hush settled over the small crowd. I welcomed the silence. Before they could ask more questions, Finn suggested that we leave. After paying our bills, Finn went to work. I walked back to this small cabin with nothing to do but wait for backup and write about the past.

\*\*\*

In the final three days of the fishing season, only two eight-hour fishing windows opened. Both the *Mikilak* and the *Nereid* hauled in average loads. Disappointment hung over the bay like the clouds that enveloped the region.

The season was a bust for everyone except for me and Joe and a few other boats. Shenan and I wore pieces of netting around our fingers in lieu of actual rings. Shenan made them. "They don't seem very permanent," I said.

"Nothing is, Jim. Enjoy the net while you're in it."

"I'll get you a real ring when we get back to civilization."

"Who says I want one?"

Sharing the news of our engagement with our skippers, Phillip complained that Shenan's parents were going to banish him from the family. Still, he didn't seem genuinely upset. In fact, I sensed both he and Joe were pleased.

Upon returning to Dillingham, we met with the pastor of the local Moravian Church and married two days later. A few guests came, including Phillip and Joe, and several fishermen that we knew. I bought a button-up shirt, and someone loaned me a blazer. Shenan wore her short gypsy dress with a white sweater. It was the closest thing she had to a wedding dress.

We kissed and walked through a shower of rice, then went to the cannery to make a phone call. When it started to rain, Shenan commented how lucky we were that the weather had waited till the end of our wedding.

The pay phone hung on the outside of the cannery under a small plywood overhang. Fishermen and cannery workers waited in line as the two of us tucked under the roof. Shenan called her parents. She told her mother she had big news and that she wanted her father to pick up the other line. When he did, she told them she was a married woman. There was silence, then questions—mostly about me. Shenan portrayed me as a charming college student with a healthy Protestant work ethic and strong moral values. We might stay in Alaska for a while, she said, then she would change her enrollment to the University of Washington where we would finish college together. She said this to please them, but our future was far from determined. She assured them that she would call again when we arrived safely in Homer and that she would share more of our plans at that time.

She hung up the phone to make way for the next guy in line. We dashed out of the plywood overhang with our jackets over our heads as the rain muddied the streets around us. "Were they mad?" I asked.

"Maybe a little, but more worried. They said they were happy for me, though. And they were surprised, of course. To be honest, I think they were only upset about not being here, and I wish they could have been." Shenan wiped her cheek, either from the rain or tears, or both.

Time phased into a blur. I asked Shenan if it felt the same for her. Since she never expected to live past her twenties, she said, she always felt life rushing hurriedly by her. The only remedy, she explained, was to stop and feel each moment of every day. "Life is measured in moments of awareness, Jim, not lineal time. Someday, I will teach you more about mindfulness. A lifetime can be lived in a day."

A few tasks, at least, were known entities. Shenan served as a deckhand on her uncle's boat, and that boat belonged in Homer, on the other side of the Alaska Peninsula. While the *Mikilak* always wintered in Dillingham, near Joe's village, the *Nereid,* like many other boats, belonged to a different city. Shenan arrived with Phillip by motoring around the Peninsula, but Phillip, concerned about the engine trouble, decided to return via an unorthodox route. Rather than sailing hundreds of miles west around the peninsula before heading back east, many boats now used the portage road between Lake Iliamna and Cook Inlet. By motoring up the Kvichak River, crossing the seventy-mile lake to Pile Bay, then hauling the boat via truck over a fifteen-mile road, one could shave a thousand miles off the journey. The portage is a poor man's Panama Canal, and it works beautifully, but nothing had prompted Phillip to try it until now. My employment with Joe was done for the season, so I volunteered to ride with Phillip and Shenan across the portage to Homer. We waited for the new head gasket to arrive, and that gave me just the right amount of time for something important.

"You ready?" I asked Shenan when I returned to our stale-smelling room in the cheap hotel. The place was better suited to transients waiting for a flight out of town than to a newlywed couple.

"For what?" She had been coughing, and I surmised that she had just gone through a major fit while I was out running errands.

"Our honeymoon, of course."

"Oh, you mean we get to have a real one?"

"What's the benefit of working on one of the top-paying boats if you stay in a place like this? We're leaving in an hour, if that's alright with you."

"Of course! How long will we be gone?"

"Two days."

"What about my uncle?"

"I already talked to him. He's cool with it. He's going to work on the engine while we're away. He knows where we're going and how to get ahold of us."

"I don't suppose you're going to tell me where we're going."

"I'll just say that first we're going to a place called Shannon's Pond."

"Ooh, did they name it after me?"

"Of course, but we'll have to tell them that they spelled it wrong."

We packed a few bags, including Shenan's guitar, and caught a ride in a tiny Datsun pickup to the pond. I don't remember the name of the man who gave us the ride, but he was fat enough to fill half the cabin by himself. Shenan had to squeeze tight against him so I could latch the door.

"I hope you don't mind cuddling," the bearded man said, shifting gears between Shenan's legs.

I wondered then if he would have given me a ride if I was alone. The entire trip was a laugh, especially as we bounced ludicrously over the bumps and potholes. Shenan's body went limp with laughing so hard. Eventually, the man began laughing with us, especially when I hit my head on the ceiling. After that, I think he went fast and purposefully hit the deepest holes. Arriving at the pond, we thanked him and offered him a few dollars that he wouldn't accept. "Are you kidding me?" he said. "That's the most fun I've had in three months."

As the tiny pick-up puttered away, Shenan continued to laugh. "Well, that was an adventure."

"And we might be doing it again in a few days."

"I bet he's hoping that we are."

We turned toward the pond and started walking.

"What is this place?"

"Float planes take off and land here. It's my personal opinion that you haven't experienced Alaska if you haven't been in a small plane."

About a half-dozen other planes floated on the pond. We carried our things down to a dock and climbed aboard a red de Havilland Beaver—the old kind, with a piston engine and a round nose. I offered Shenan the front seat, but she insisted that I sit there.

After donning our headgear, the pilot throttled the engine into a raucous roar, and we skidded across the pond until we escaped the drag of the water and lifted into the air. Passing over the treetops, Shenan watched out the window with her fingertips pressed to the glass. She was, of course, a woman, but still a child, too. At altitude, we talked by pulling our ear protection away from our heads and leaning close. "We're going to a lake—the biggest lake in all of Alaska," I explained. "It's the same lake we're going to cross with the *Nereid*. I got us a room in a lodge—a nice one, I think—so we can have a proper honeymoon."

She clasped her hands in front of her chest. "That sounds perfect, Jim."

"I wanted you to have the experience of flying in a sea plane, and there's one more thing—something that you told me you wanted to see."

She raised an eyebrow. "What is it?"

"Just wait. I'll let you know if I see it."

Fifteen minutes later, I turned to Shenan and pointed out the right side of the aircraft. From the expression on her face I could see that she didn't know what she was looking at—lines of light tan specks weaving across the ground like a braided river. At first, it was just a few lines, then these lines melded into a vast horde of light tan specks that covered the ground beneath us as far as we could see.

"Is that what I think it is?"

"Yes, caribou."

"There must be thousands of them."

"Hundreds of thousands," the pilot interjected.

We watched the vast heard stretch on as we passed over it. We pressed our foreheads to the cold glass while the engine droned loudly in front of us. I thought of an old Inuit legend I had once read. In it, a man who lived long ago dug a deep hole in the ground. Out of the ground poured caribou from a supply that seemed inexhaustible. Once he thought there was enough caribou on the earth for mankind, he closed the hole again, but by the time he covered the hole, the earth was covered in caribou. The sight below almost proved the myth. The caribou seemed inexhaustible—even from the sky.

The pilot dipped the wings, so we could look at the caribou right below us. Turning toward Shenan, I lifted an earmuff from one ear and yelled, "What do you think?"

"It makes me feel that humans are a minority," she said, still peering down at them and speaking loudly over the engine. Then, in a voice so quiet I had to read her lips, she added, "and that I am just a tiny speck on this planet."

I nodded.

Some minutes later, we passed beyond sight of them. The pilot asked if I would like to take the stick for a while. "Sure," I said, chomping at the bit. He pulled the release knob on the center stem and arced the throwover yoke to a position in front of me. I took the controls in both hands. Before I even had time to think about it, I was flying. The pilot reached over and with a little pressure on my hand gently dipped the wings left and right in slow, graceful turns.

Shenan leaned forward in her seat, placed her hand on my shoulder, and watched. "You look like a natural."

"Thanks," I said, "but I don't feel like one." The pilot allowed me to make small corrections on my own and I felt the aircraft respond just as I had expected. After five minutes or so, I relinquished control to the pilot who pulled the release knob and returned the yoke to the left side. It was my first real taste of flying, and it left a deep impression.

While I had flown in small planes several times, I had never landed in the water. My first thought while dropping toward the water at high speed was that the floats would catch in the water and flip us over. Surely, we were going too fast, I thought. The lake seemed to approach us from the bottom, not the other way around. I glanced back at Shenan who clutched the seat beneath her. I turned and did the same as the water rose up toward us. Contrary to my expectations, our first contact with the water barely slowed us down and we bounced briefly back into the air. It felt something like the end of a roller coaster as the hills get smaller and your speed diminishes. When the floats stopped planing on the surface and settled into the water, it was a let-down both physical and emotional. I immediately wanted to return to the air again. Instead, we taxied to a dock near a magnificent lodge. The pilot handed our bags to us and said he would see us in a few days.

We climbed up stone steps set into the bank and went inside. "Will you be fishing?" the man behind the desk asked.

"No, we just caught a million fish," I said. "This is our honeymoon, actually."

"Oh," he said, his hard demeanor relaxing a bit. "Well, you won't find any heart-shaped beds here, but I'll put you in our room with the best view."

"Thank you," I said. "That's all we want."

We did a great deal during those two days in the lodge. We sat in the sauna behind the building. Shenan sang songs for me on the deck overlooking the lake. We played games and shared stories from our childhoods. She wrapped herself in the wolf skin that covered the bed and pretended to howl. In bed, she taught me how she liked to be touched.

"I don't want this to end," I told her as we lay in bed looking at one another.

A smile crept across her face. "It doesn't have to," she said.

"What do you mean?"

She sat up enthusiastically. "I'm going to teach you something." She was naked, so she slipped on her underwear and the long john shirt, then sat in the bed with her legs crossed in front of her. "Now sit up and do what I'm doing."

"What *are* we doing?"

"I'm going to teach you about mindfulness."

I did as she asked, pulling the blanket over my lap, and sat facing her with my legs crossed.

"Put your hands on your knees like this and touch your fingertips together."

"How's this?"

"Good."

"Now close your eyes. I want you to let go of all the thoughts in your mind. Stop thinking about the past. Stop thinking about the future. Think only of the present moment. Just listen to my voice or concentrate on your own breaths." She looked so appealing in her outfit that it was hard to concentrate. "Now, I'm going to count backwards from thirty. As I count, slowly and purposefully relax every muscle in your body, starting from the top and working down. By the time I reach the number one, you should have relaxed every muscle in your body, and you should be thinking only of the present moment. We will then go into a minute of silence. During that minute, I want you to be aware of nothing but the breaths coming in and out of your body. Listen to them and think about how they sound and how easily they pass in and out. If a thought enters your mind, acknowledge it, then let it pass away. We're going to sit there like that for a minute and think of nothing but our breathing. Are you ready?"

"Yes."

Shenan started counting. With my eyes closed, I did my best to follow her instructions. When we reached our minute of silence, my mind settled into a wonderful place, but I knew I wasn't doing what I had been told. I didn't think about my breathing. My mind was not empty. I opened my eyes and looked at the peaceful face of the woman in front of me. I thought about how lucky I was to be there in that moment, how lucky I was to be alive, and to be young, and to be married to this amazing woman, how thankful I was that she was still alive, and that someday, perhaps soon, she wouldn't be, but that she was here with me now. I knew I had to appreciate that fact, and be perfectly happy with who I was, where I was, and who I was with. Though I didn't follow her instructions exactly, my thoughts centered me in the present, even if it was a present considered in the context of the future, and it made me appreciate the present more than ever. Before the minute expired, I closed my eyes again, so she couldn't see that I had been cheating. When it was over, she asked me how I felt.

"Lucky to be alive," I said, studying her face, trying to memorize every detail of it, "and thankful that I'm right here in this moment."

"Really?"

"Yes."

She put her hand on the blanket over my knee. "You're a quick learner, Jim LaBerg."

On our second night, as we lay under the blankets and the wolf skin, she propped herself up on an elbow, facing me. "Jim, there's something I need to share with you."

"This sounds serious."

"It is very serious, but don't worry—it's all good, I think.  And it's definitely not certain."

"Okay."

"When you asked me to marry you, do you remember me saying that it wasn't just about my dreams . . . that I also wanted to make your dreams come true?"

"Yes."

"That's good, because one of your long-term dreams might be coming true."

"What's that?"

She pulled away slightly and looked me directly in the eyes.  In them, I saw both hope and fear.  "I'm late in my cycle."

It took several seconds for the full weight of her words to hit me.  "Ah, I see.  So soon?"

"Maybe.  At first, I thought I was just a few days off, but now I don't think so."

A spark erupted deep within my chest that exploded into butterflies that descended to my stomach.  We had briefly talked about using protection when we got married but determined to leave it to fate.  Besides, she felt that her condition made her less fertile.  That's what her doctors told her, anyway.  But it had only been several weeks since we made love after our encounter with the wolves, so it must have happened the first time.

"Do you really think so?"

"I don't know for sure, but I have thought so for several days now. You know how I didn't want that omelet when we got here?"

"Yes."

"I hated the onions for some reason, and I normally love onions." There was a pause, then she said, "You don't look happy."

"I am happy. My first thought was a happy one, a very happy one . . ."

"But then?"

"I worried about your health."

She grimaced, causing her chin to crinkle. "Yes, there is that. But you said that faith the size of a mustard seed can move mountains, didn't you?"

"I did say that, didn't I." I hugged her tightly. "I'll say this—it's going to be an adventure."

"I won't let your life get boring, Jim LaBerg, at least not for a while."

"Not for a long while," I added.

"Not for a long while," she repeated, but she didn't sound convinced.

# Chapter 18

# Peace, Be Still

I often find myself reliving those moments, especially while flying over this place called The Great Land. I sometimes wish that time could have stopped during our stay in that lodge, but the future comes whether we like it or not. We had so many decisions to make about the future—to stay in Alaska or to go back to college, to raise a baby in a college town or in the wilderness, whether Shenan should continue her studies or stay at home. We also considered whether Shenan had to live close to her team of doctors in Virginia. She didn't think so. I wasn't so sure.

Despite all the questions, we mostly tried to ignore the future. Besides, we had to motor the *Nereid* to Homer first. This multifaceted route comprised a 50-mile trip up the Kvichak River, a 70-mile voyage across the very lake where we had just been staying, and a 15-mile road trip on a truck over the portage road to Williamsport. Once settling the *Nereid* in the water again, we had to steam another 70 miles across the Cook Inlet to Homer. At the very least, the detailed plan gave our lives some semblance of direction for the next few weeks.

On our flight back to Dillingham, I insisted that Shenan sit up front. We saw less caribou but sighted a bear with two cubs. Back in Dillingham, we found that Phillip had received the correct head gasket and had replaced it with help from one of the *Lucky Linda's* crewmembers. There was a noticeable improvement, he said, especially at low RPMs. Phillip briefly considered going back the way he had come, but the marine radio now warned that a storm was developing over the Bering Sea and growing in intensity. Its current location was hundreds of miles away, but forecasters advised that persons in Bristol Bay should prepare for a high-magnitude storm within days. Fortunately, the Kvichak River route led us away from the bad weather.

Phillip restocked the boat with food and gas and reconnoitered the new route by asking others who had made the portage trip before. He learned where the shallows were in the river and the best route across the lake to the truck haul-out on Pile Bay. If the storm ever did come east, we would be well on the other side of the Peninsula, or at least in the relative security of Lake Iliamna.

We offered to help Joe winterize the *Mikilak*, which would spend the cold months on stilts in the boatyard, but he still needed it to haul winter supplies to his cabin. There was a third boat I had to attend to. Nearby, the salmon-colored boat sat perched on high ground with the *For Sale* sign in the window. Shenan and I stuffed the cushion back into the duffel bag and snuck it back to the boat late at night when it was almost dark. It was now locked, likely due to the detected theft, so we wrapped the cushion in a few garbage bags and stowed it in the fish hold. Shenan looked in the windows. It was a beautiful boat. We discussed how fishing in the summer would give us cash to supplement our lives in the wilderness. She liked the idea, so long as it didn't interfere with the completion of my degree.

Phillip was in a hurry. The Bering Sea was reportedly getting thrashed by the storm, which was already pushing water into the Bay. Its wind licked us from far away. Arms of rain touched us in alternating wet and dry spells. We said our good-byes to Joe. He was more than a boss to me—he had been a father figure—and I felt oddly adrift at the thought of navigating Alaska without him.

We embraced. I told him that if all went well, we would see each other again next summer. He kissed Shenan on the cheek, then told her to take care of the little one. She glanced at me, wondering if I had told him. I shook my head. She touched the front of her foul weather gear. "I will, Joe. I'll do the best that I can."

We donned our jackets when the rain picked up again. A loud cacophony of constant clicks tapped on the plastic hoods around our ears. We could only hear each other if we yelled, so we spoke only when necessary. As we pulled away from the pier, the wind sucked Shenan's hair out of her hood as if it were trying to pull her out of our dimension. She smiled at me through the confused tangle, which reminded me of the first time I saw her, only two months earlier.

When I turned into the wind, it beat cold against my chest. It came from the west, and it was only a matter of time before it brought the weather from the brutal Bering Sea. As Shenan and I tidied the mooring lines, Phillip turned the boat's nose into the chop and pushed south out of the harbor.

With everything secured, Shenan and I went into the cabin with Phillip. The cranberry float was there. Not long after Shenan had given it to me, I hung it in a small piece of netting in the corner of the *Mikilak's* pilothouse. When we switched boats, I moved it to a similar position in the *Nereid*. Now it slid back and forth across the wall next to Phillip. By the time we passed into the open bay an hour later, it gyrated alarmingly as we moved into the deep swells that had been generated by the storm to the west. I removed it from the wall and placed it among the coffee mugs in the sink. Throughout the cabin, Shenan and I picked up loose gear and stowed it wherever we could.

We plowed through the waves, listening to the radio. The storm moved up the bay, pushing a million cubic feet of water ahead of it. Forecasters warned that as the water passed into the narrower regions of the bay it would flood low-lying structures. Wind gusts of sixty to eighty miles per hour had already been reported west of Cape Menshikof. The three of us were anxious to get around Clark's Point and head east into the relative safety of the Kvichak River. Phillip advised us that we would seek safety in the somewhat sheltered harbors of

Naknek or King Salmon should the storm arrive sooner than predicted. We turned off the radio when the reports grew repetitive. As imposing as the waves were, I knew the *Nereid* could weather a storm such as this. Gillnetting boats were designed to handle rough weather. I wanted to make more coffee but knew the careening of the boat precluded a hot kettle on the stove. I sat stretched on the galley bench across from Shenan while Phillip manned the helm. Rain and sea-spray pummeled the windshield. The wipers barely kept up.

As the hours wore on, the waves intensified, and the wind grew dangerously strong. The storm was catching us. For the first time in my life, my stomach grew queasy as the drenching, numbing feeling of seasickness poured over me. I glanced at Shenan who sat motionless with her temple glued to the glass. Her lifeless features and pale skin suggested that nausea had descended on her as well.

The rain pelted our windshield, but it was nothing compared to the barrage of water that enveloped us every time the bow crashed into the troughs. The boat trembled.

Phillip eyed the fathometer carefully, its red traces assuring us that we were not among the shallow sandbars. In those days, radars were not common. We relied on charts, compasses, fathometers, and most of all, personal knowledge of the Bay.

Another hour slipped by and I grew accustomed to the commotion around us. After shattering a hundred burly waves I knew the *Nereid* could take them. However, I grew increasingly sick and wanted more than anything for the queasiness to go away. I rested my chin on my outstretched arm. My hand lay on Shenan's forearm. She sat across the table doing the same thing, keeping still as possible, with her hand on top of mine. I watched the water froth outside the window then leaned my head against the glass and closed my eyes. I wondered at the fact that a quarter-inch piece of glass was all that protected us from the mayhem. To take my mind off the growing sickness, I thought about my life with Shenan. For two seconds my heart thrilled. Then, rather unexpectedly, my heart plunged as our boat slid down the backside of a wave and I realized I had two lives to worry about. No, three. No longer did the expression "Every Man to Himself" apply. I had a wife—a pregnant wife—and two lives to put before my own. I looked at her. She looked at me with uneasy eyes. I smiled to reassure her.

The thought struck me then how little I knew her. How did this woman, who I did not know two months before, become my wife? I knew that I had been impulsive. I allowed myself to be. I did so because she was dying. She was never *really* going to live in a cabin, was she? Was she healthy enough to have a baby? My stomach lurched. I grabbed a pot and vomited into it. My body tingled in unpleasant ways. I distinctly remember staring into the pan, at my own vomit, enjoying the few seconds of relief before the sickness crawled over my body again. I sat there, slightly trembling, when the engine stuttered and I wondered if it was just some trick of my imagination.

As slowly as I could, I looked up at Phillip who modulated the throttle carefully while the engine picked up speed, then choked, then resumed normal speed again. "That's interesting," Phillip said in glaring understatement. "I've noticed she's still been doing that at high RPM."

It stuttered again.

"You've noticed this before?"

He looked at me, and for the first time ever I saw fear in his eyes—small and minute, but perceptible. "It's still better than it was before," he said.

The engine choked again.

"I'd better take a look."

He motioned for me to take the helm. I summoned every ounce of energy in my body, which had been drained by seasickness. I didn't look at Shenan because I didn't think I could muster an authentic smile at the time. I stumbled across the swaying deck and took the helm. "Steer clear of the Sands," Phillip said pointing through the film of water to some poorly defined gray area ahead and to the left.

"Deadman's Sands?"

He didn't answer. The name, Deadman's Sands, had always sounded romantic. It didn't now.

The engine stuttered again, and I wiggled the throttle like Phillip had done. Though I didn't know why, it seemed to help.

Donning his foul weather jacket, Phillip grabbed the toolbox from under the bench. The engine stalled. Not stuttered—stalled. Immediately, our bow turned away from the waves without any propulsion to guide her. I placed the gearbox lever in neutral and hit the start button. After a few seconds, the engine sputtered to a slow idle, coughing slightly, protesting that it wanted to sleep. We floated nearly abreast of the waves and the boat rolled alarmingly. Phillip braced himself with one hand on the bulkhead and the other on the table. He watched as I increased the throttle. The engine responded appropriately, and I soon had enough power to turn the nose into the waves again. Facing the power of the waves, I pushed the lever to full throttle. The engine stuttered, retorting against the load, and died again.

For the second time in as many minutes, we were adrift in a storm, drifting ever closer to Deadman's Sands. The *Nereid* rolled deeply onto her port side and I remember looking out the left window almost directly down to the water. When she crested the wave and lurched to the right, Phillip and Shenan clutched the table to prevent from being thrown.

With one hand, I repeated my previous actions. The engine started again, the most reassuring sound I had ever heard. I brought the engine to half-throttle with trepidation. She didn't like full power—that I had learned—so I didn't push it. She stuttered but stayed alive. Immediately, I spun the helm hard-over to starboard. At half-power, the boat crept slowly to the right, eventually holding her nose in the weather again. Half power was not enough to make forward progress, but it was enough to keep us from blowing toward the sand bars. Phillip's eyes darted out the port windows, causing me to do the same. The shore was a half-mile away. But the problem wasn't the shore. The problem was a long stretch of hidden sandbars that lay between us and the shore. In fact, in very low tides, these sandbars transformed into long, flat islands. Just when I thought dry land was the one thing I wanted more than anything else, the sight of that low rise frightened me more than any sea monster could have.

"Keep it at half throttle and hold us here!" Phillip yelled over the sound of the wind and the waves. "I'm going to have a look! It seems we're starving for fuel!" I glanced at the gas gauge which showed we had plenty in the tank. I nodded my head as he opened the door and breached the threshold of the storm. The door slammed behind him. I watched him lurch back and forth across the deck, cross the fish hold on all fours, push the net aside and unscrew the engine cover through an inch of sloshing water. In less than a minute, Phillip's head and shoulders disappeared into the engine hold.

I turned to Shenan.

"So, it's not fixed after all?" she asked.

"Apparently not."

Her eyes grew wet and the color drained from her cheeks. "Are we in serious danger?" She braced one hand against the cushions while the other still clutched the table. The boat rose and plunged like a cheap carnival ride.

"These boats can handle a storm like this, as long as the engine works."

"I see," she said, turning to view her uncle, biting her lower lip.

I returned my eyes to the sea.

We rose quickly over a wave and plunged down the backside. The ocean tossed the *Nereid* like a strongman throwing a kettlebell and sickness overwhelmed me again. I turned and vomited in the sink. I prayed for our safety while adjusting the rudder to keep us pointed away from land and the invisible bars below. The engine sputtered many times, threatening to give up completely.

Then it did.

I went through the motions like a robot, trying to attach no importance to their outcome—gearbox in neutral, throttle down, start button. Nothing. The bow swung away from the incessant waves. I tried again with less throttle. She came to life, but life on the verge of death. I had barely enough power to steer the boat, and we moved incrementally backward.

Phillip returned to the cabin soaked. He pulled his hood behind his wet hair and yelled, "It's the fuel filter!" I looked back at him waiting for him to elaborate. "Which is odd," he continued, "because I just put the new one in a month ago."

"What do you mean, 'the new one'?"

"The old one went foul, so I put the spare in."

"Do we have another spare?" I asked, not wanting to hear the answer.

"No. Two should have been more than enough to last us a very long time! That's what I can't understand. It's really dirty. There's something in the tank," he said, stomping on the deck below us.

The engine coughed like a diseased old woman. "Now what?!" I yelled.

"We can't go on like this," he said. He looked over his back at the slowly approaching banks. "We're not holding our position. There's sandbars out here."

"I know that!" I yelled, thinking that this would have never happened with Joe. Joe understood the factors that meant the difference between life and death, about having a back-up to a back-up and a plan behind that. One bad factor, such as a storm, will jeopardize you. Add a second factor, such as clogged fuel filter, and you will be placed in grave danger. Add a third factor, such as the lack of a spare, and you may very well die. If your car engine dies on the road, you pull over and wait for help. But the sea is not like that. The sea is always trying to kill you. Phillip thought a second more. "I'm going to bypass the filter."

"Okay," I said, trying to sound calm. "Good idea. Will the fuel line reach the carburetor?"

"No, I already checked. It's six inches too short."

A wave as tall as the boat lifted our bow in the air until we pointed toward the sky. I held onto the helm so that I wouldn't fall against the back wall. Phillip's grip on the counter slipped and he was thrown against the aft wall next to Shenan. She reached to help him. The wave did not topple us, but it threw our boat twenty yards closer to the shore. *Six inches too short!* I told myself. *Six inches?!* I screamed in my head. *We're in danger of losing everything because of six inches!*

Phillip righted himself when the monster wave passed. He stumbled toward the galley drawers next to me, unlatched one of them, and fumbled through a mess of 12-volt wire, kitchen caulk, pliers, and a myriad other things. He turned and said sharply, "Get on the radio and get some help."

I unclipped the transceiver and brought it to my mouth. I paused, trying to think of what to say. I squeezed the button. "Is anyone out there? This is the *Nereid*."

Phillip jerked the transceiver from my hand and brought it to his lips. "Mayday. Mayday. Mayday. This is the *Nereid*. We are near the north shore of Kvichak Bay, approximately thirty miles from the mouth of the Kvichak River. Our engine has stalled. We need emergency assistance."

As he spoke, he grabbed a roll of black electric tape. He handed the transceiver back to me and said, "I'm going to splice the two hoses together."

A good idea, I thought, but it would take time. Yet, as our boat slid ever closer to the shore and even closer to the hidden sandbars, I knew it was our only choice. The most troubling question of all was the one I asked next. "How long will I have to turn off the engine?"

"Only a minute," Phillip said.

"What?" I yelled, turning my ear toward him.

He placed his hand on my shoulder. "Only a minute!" he yelled into my left ear. "When I'm ready, I'll motion for you to cut it! When I'm done, I'll give you a thumbs up! Okay?"

My stomach cramped. I couldn't make it to the sink in time. I vomited right on the floor. I showed him a thumbs-up. Another large wave thrust us back. Phillip stumbled left and right as he donned his hood and went out into the storm.

"Are you okay, Jim?" Shenan asked, speaking loudly over the pummeling of the rain against the glass. She scooted to the edge of the bench and reached for my hand. I reached and gave her hand a squeeze before returning both hands to the helm, which required constant adjustment.

"Yes, baby," I said, though I felt far from okay.

"The storm came so fast."

"I know. That was faster than they said." A voice came over the radio, asking to repeat the last call. I did my best to say exactly what Phillip had said. "We'll head your way," the voice replied, "but it will take twenty to thirty."

"Understood," I said. "Come as fast as you can."

I watched Phillip remove the engine cover. "Let's pray," I said, reaching toward Shenan again. She took my hand. "Father," I said, with my eyes open, waiting for Phillip's signal. "Father, protect your children in this hour of need. Give Phillip wisdom. Guide us safely to port."

"Amen," Shenan said, squeezing my hand before letting go. I felt more confident and I wondered if it was due to the prayer, the knowledge that help was on its way, or the squeeze of Shenan's hand.

I pulled my small Bible from the shelf an arm's-length from me. The pots and pans clanged in the sink along with the cranberry float. My stomach was sore from vomiting. The rain and sea-spray covered the windows to the point of blindness, and waves slammed the bow of our little boat sending tremors through the fiberglass hull. Our engine sputtered constantly while it worked to stay alive. We had no power to speed away from the danger, and our skipper was head-and-shoulders in the belly of our boat exposed to all of nature's elements as well as the bite of our own engine.

I opened the window a sliver so the storm could hear me. It reached in and touched me with icy fingers, but I wanted it to hear what I had to say when I cut the engine. Phillip's head emerged from the engine compartment. He gave me the signal. I hit the kill switch. The engine stopped. We were adrift. But I didn't fear the storm. With one hand on the useless wheel, I opened my Bible instinctively to Mark, chapter four, and read.

*"And there arose a great storm of wind, and the waves beat into the ship, so that it was now full. And he was in the hinder part of the ship, asleep on a pillow: and they awake him, and say unto him, Master, carest thou not that we perish? And he arose, and rebuked the wind, and said unto the sea, Peace, be still. And the wind ceased, and there was a great calm."*

As I read the last sentence, a wave picked us up and dropped us like a pan with a hot handle. We hit solid ground. Nearly everything in the cabin, including me, was thrown against the port wall. A pot hit me in the eye and gashed my forehead. My immediate thought was to get back to the helm to control the boat, then realized it was useless. Water poured in from somewhere, maybe everywhere. We rose briefly from the trough and were temporarily afloat. The bow veered quickly to the left and I knew we were about to be thrown again. We plunged, then landed, and the hull cracked. We rose again. I righted myself in the spinning room now filling with blindingly cold water and struggled to Shenan's arms.

"We have to get out!" I opened the cabin door, pulling against a strong current of water. Phillip had fallen deeper into the engine hold and was struggling to get out.

With the boat spinning on its axis, I took Shenan's hand and helped her out the door. The freezing water reached to our waists. Then the boat lifted again, and the water fled as quickly as it had come. I moved toward Phillip. We were now completely abreast of the waves and I found myself looking down a long sea-trough that looked like a sunlit valley between two mountainous waves. For a momentary flash, the scene looked beautiful and tranquil. "Peace. Be still," I said.

We rose high on a crest, then plummeted fast until we hit the bar again. I felt Shenan's fingers slip from my own as the boat rolled into a wall of water. In an instant, it was all around us. The cold took my breath away and tightened my muscles into useless knots. I remember surfacing to the sight of the *Nereid* rolling end over end as the waves tumbled her across the sandbar. I swam toward the boat first, looking for Shenan, but the waves pulled on my heavy clothes. Soon, my only thought was to keep my head above the surface. The sight of the not-so-distant shore was my friend again. Unexpectedly, my boots hit solid ground. The last thing I remember is the sight of the grass—the beautiful, waving grass—and I half-swam, half-waded toward it with every shred of willpower that I could muster.

# Chapter 19

# The Muddy Grays of Life

I shivered in pain. I was awake, but barely. A spasm of muscle contractions passed over my body and awoke me further. My body threatened to rattle itself apart. My arms and neck twisted into knots. Before I opened my eyes, I tasted the gritty mud in my mouth and remembered where I was, vaguely, and what had happened.

Opening my eyes, I saw a long strand of muddy beach stretching into the distance. A few feet above me, the tundra sedge sat motionless, and several feet below me, the water licked gently at the shore in an unthreatening manner. The sun, either setting or rising, gave the sky a cold, weak color. My body ached with cold. I prayed the sun was rising instead of setting. If it was setting,

I knew that greater suffering awaited me in the night. Though it was the middle of the summer, this wasn't Shenan's Eastern Shore. It was Alaska, and in Alaska hypothermia is always lurking around the corner. In a moment of rational thought, I remembered that we were on the north shore of Kvichak Bay, and the weak sun lay low in the west. It was setting. I had to get up and move, but the energy wasn't there until I thought about Shenan. I started to pray, then felt a pervasive numbness of the soul when I realized how useless my praying had been some hours before.

Only eight weeks prior, I had gone to bed in the bow of the *Mikilak* a sure, confident man. I awoke every morning with the comforting knowledge that the world followed a specific set of rules and I knew the rules. I had prayed for a job in Alaska and found the Bible Camp. I had prayed for the opportunity to go fishing and found that. Even recently, the rules made sense. My wife was sick, but I had convinced myself that God would heal her. And when he did, I believed that she would find faith.

But on that morning, on that dirty, lifeless beach, I awoke to the muddy grays of life. The world, now, was as big as the sky—the tepid, gray sky, so much bigger than me, so uncaring about me, sitting over the calm water that now looked untouched, unbothered by the storm. Neither the water nor the sky cared about my faith, my prayers, my struggles, my dreams. My faith could not tame them. I was not their master. I wasn't even their toy. I was just another piece of driftwood lying on the edge of an icy, senseless shore. Only one hope remained, and that was to find Shenan alive.

I rose to my elbows and knees. My clothes—caked with mud in places, still wet in others—clung to my body like an old layer of skin needing to be shed. Leaning on my arms, I looked down the shoreline and saw the *Nereid* only a hundred yards away. Between me and the boat, debris lay scattered, some of it still floating in the low tide, the rest strewn up and down the beach. The *Nereid*'s hull lay upside-down in the mud, her cabin shorn off by the sandbar. I pressed my aching head with my hands and felt sand and crusted blood, then remembered getting struck by the pot.

I tried to stand, but fierce cramps immediately forced me to a knee. I yelled through clenched teeth, desperately trying to garner the energy to find Phillip and Shenan. I stood again—this time slowly—stretching my arms and legs, pulling purposefully against the kinks. My limbs shivered profusely, but the spasms abated.

I walked first, then jogged down the beach past familiar things—pieces of the cabin, a net strung out between the water and the shore, boxes of Pilot crackers, a jar of jelly, boat fenders, and the cranberry float bobbing near the shore.

I reached the hull of the *Nereid* seeing no sign of the other two. Out of breath and weary, I rested my hand on the keel. The green slime that coated the bottom of the boat had already dried into a rough texture on the fiberglass. Phillip meant to raise her from the water to clean her for some time, but never got around to it.

Bracing myself against the hull, I stepped gently around what remained of the boat, trying hard to avoid the broken fiberglass and the sharp planks of wood and that jutted from underneath. I made it to the bow, which pointed toward higher ground, and looked around the other side. There was Shenan—lying on her back just above the waterline. The overturned boat lay on top of her, leaving only her head, shoulder and an arm exposed. She didn't move. Her eyes stared blankly at the sky. I rushed to her side, stumbling over more debris, slicing my shin on a nail. I called her name, then bent close to her.

"Shenan. Shenan. Can you hear me?" I cradled her head. Her cold, black hair covered her mouth. I wiped it away. Her cheeks were ice cold. I rubbed them. I looked down the beach and saw Phillip's body lying face down in the mud.

"Shenan!" I cried louder.

When I first saw her, I think I knew instinctively that she was dead, but once I started talking, something snapped in my mind and she seemed alive again. My primary thought was to get the boat off her. Her lower body was probably in the freezing water, and cold water kills quickly. My mind focused on making her warm.

"Hold on, Shenan," I yelled as I braced my back against the hull and crouched until my hands slid under the gunnel. I pressed my damp hiking boots into the mud, and with all my might strained to lift the hull. Of course, there was not the slightest hint of movement. The boat weighed a thousand pounds and it was half-buried in the mud, but rationality had left me. I looked at Shenan, her hair in the mud, her lifeless eyes staring at the sky. Her eyes were dry. Still, I envisioned life in them. Perhaps she was in the advanced stages of hypothermia, I told myself. I had to get her into the sun. I had to build a fire. Fire was the only thing that would save us.

I strained again for thirty seconds or more, gritting my teeth and peering into the clouds above. The plan to build a fire inspired me. The clouds opened a momentary hole, and the sunlight grew incrementally brighter. It felt like a sign. I cheered myself on. "Okay, Jim, you've got this. One, two, *three*!" I lifted with all my might, my legs trembling with the effort.

I cannot recall how long I carried on like this, nor do I care to. It was many minutes, perhaps a quarter of an hour. I reached down to touch Shenan's cheek, told her to keep praying and that I would get her out. I told her I would find some matches. I told her I would build a fire. "Imagine how good that's going to feel," I said. I counted again before straining with all my might. I was certain I could move the boat. It was not that big—I had seen it bob like a feather on the water. I had pushed it from the dock with one hand. I couldn't believe it was heavy as concrete now.

Small troughs developed around my boots where they shoveled up the silty mud. My back ached, and pains spread through my groin. I pushed and screamed again, though my body was nearly too depleted to stand. I no longer used energy to support my back and torso. I let my body grow limp, focusing only on the muscles in my fingers and thighs.

"Okay, Shenan," I said. My breathing had grown heavy, nearly to the point of passing out. "I felt it move that time. When it lifts, pull yourself out. Ready? One, two, *three!*" I screamed at the sky through clenched teeth, diverting all my energy to my legs, then something stabbed me in my right groin. I released the boat and reached down my pants toward the pain. With tears in my eyes, I felt a large lump near the crease of my upper thigh. There was a smaller one on the other side. I knew enough to know they were hernias. "Damn!" I yelled. I looked at Shenan's lifeless body and reason returned to me in the middle of the pain and the heavy breathing. Shenan was dead. I felt the larger bulge on the right side again. "Damn! Damn! Damn!" Then, more quietly, "Look at what you've done."

I determined to push the larger hernia back in. I thought it would be safer that way. I pushed until I could not bear the pain. My body shut down and everything went black.

\*\*\*

Sometime later, behind closed eyelids, I encountered Joe. "Thank God," I heard him say. His boots made a sound alternating between sucking and shifting. He was very close. "Jim," he said. "Shenan."

I imagined that Joe, Shenan and I were still together—fishing on the *Mikilak*. Except that I felt cold, very cold, and everything was sunny in my mind.

"Jim!"

"Joe?"

"Yes."

"Let Shenan sleep."

"I will."

I felt movement. Shaking. "Wake up, Jim. Wake up. Open your eyes." I couldn't. "Open your eyes! Can you move?"

I opened my eyes.

"Look at me," he said. He propped me up, then put his coat around me and rubbed it over my body. "Stay awake, Jim." Then he lifted me. I felt his cast under the crook of my knees. At some point, I was in a raft. The noisy outboard motor buzzed in my ears and vibrated through the planks below me. "Wake up, Jim. Get in the boat."

"I'm in the boat."

"No, the other boat."

"Which boat?"

"The *Mikilak*. Climb onto the *Mikilak*."

I hauled myself over the rocking gunnel of the *Mikilak* with a great deal of tugging and pushing from Joe's good arm and found myself on a familiar fish hold. Burning pain seared through my groin. "The *Mikilak?* Why are you here?"

"I came looking for you."

"Thank God you found me."

"Yes, thank God." He tied the skiff to the stern cleat.

"What about the boat that was coming?"

"They had to turn around."

"The Coast Guard?"

"They are very busy. Several boats went down."

"But you came for us."

"I heard your call. I borrowed the skiff and came for you. Let's get you warm." He led me to the pilothouse and turned the kerosene heater as high as it would go.

He crouched in front of me to adjust the blanket around my neck. He was very close. I looked him in the eyes.

"You saw the other two?" I asked.

His shoulders fell. "I saw them." His head slumped to his chest and the weight of his arms tugged at my neck as he clenched the blanket. It pulled me forward until my forehead rested on his. "We will come back for them."

"Yes, we will," I said. I started to sob.

He pressed my head against his neck and put his good arm around me. "But you're gonna make it, Jim. Let's get you to a doctor."

I awoke in the Kanakanak Hospital the next morning. I remembered the night before, laying in the hospital emergency room, listening to nurses talk about hypothermia. I remembered warm blankets placed over my body. I remembered stitches in my forehead and shin and talking to a doctor about hernias. He had said the right one needed surgery right away. We agreed to do both. They wheeled me to the operating room. When I awoke, the doctor said everything had gone well.

*Everything had not gone well,* I thought to myself sometime after the surgery. "Everything is a disaster."

"You're awake, Jim," I heard Joe say. I opened my eyes. He was sitting by my bed, his brown face placid as lake water.

"Yes."

He patted my knee. "You're going to be alright."

I asked him about Shenan and Phillip.

"They went to get them," he said, his voice more subdued.

"I see." New tears stung my eyes.

"I'm very sorry."

Quiet sobbing welled up deep within me. It made my groin hurt and my ribs ache, but it cleared my head.

"None of this makes sense, Joe."

He sat silently next to my bed with his hands folded in his lap. "What doesn't make sense?"

"All of it. Why did God bring Shenan into my life only to take her away?"

He said nothing. I sat for a minute waiting to see if he had a response while I struggled with the troubling thoughts that poisoned my mind. "I was stupid enough to think she was born with a disease to create the possibility of a miracle."

Again, he said nothing.

I explained that when I fell in love with Shenan, I prayed that she would be healed.

"We had fallen out of God's protection," I said. "That much is clear. That was my fault. We were unequally yoked. But why this?"

For every question I asked, he had no answer. I assumed that he had as many questions as I did. "Was it a test of faith? And what about the baby? That makes no sense at all. Surely, God isn't so cruel."

Joe sat so quietly that I wondered if he was really listening. Then, after a long pause, he finally spoke. "What would Shenan say?"

I thought for a moment. "That's a good question. I wish she were here so we could ask her. I loved hearing her ideas." I swallowed a sob, then ventured, "I suppose she would say it was all part of the universe's plan. That we were brought together to learn from each other, or something like that."

"Yes," he said, nodding his head slightly, "that is probably what she would say."

I pictured her talking about the universe. It briefly made me feel better. "But I don't know why the universe would do this. Is that how you feel, Joe? Do you think more like her?"

A soft breeze slid into the room from the open window behind me.

"I don't think like either of you."

I felt the breeze on my neck when I propped myself higher in the bed. I couldn't imagine what a third way of thinking would be.

"What *do* you think?"

He looked at me, his face completely devoid of emotion. "I think the fuel filter was clogged."

I scanned his weather-beaten face looking for more information.

"And the storm?"

"It was just a storm."

I leaned back and stared at the ceiling. There were tiny cracks in the plaster that I had not noticed before. They reminded me of the cracks in Michelangelo's paintings on the ceiling of the Sistine Chapel, but there was no paint here, only white plaster—white plaster with no color or embellishment. And I realized then that Joe's statement was something that Alaska had been whispering to me for some time—throughout my first summer in the mountains, my first season as a fisherman, the cold winter I spent at the Bible camp, and in the horror of the previous day. It was simply a warning, a warning that said *be careful*.

Since that day in the hospital, I have faced this fact a thousand times. Every year, boats sink, planes crash, people die on the mountain. There is always an explanation—bad weather, faulty equipment, failure to prepare, or just plain stupidity. Joe knew that. He knew that from a lifetime spent on the capricious ocean and in the bone-crushing cold of dark winters. I thought about the way he prayed. "I pray that you be with us. Thank you for dying for us. Forgive our sins." He never said, "Keep us safe. Give us lots of fish. Send good weather." I saw then that his prayers were about preparing our souls for death—sudden, unexpected, and potentially imminent, death.

More than any other place, Alaska presses this message to the front of your mind. Sometimes you look at its beauty and think that it is a land infused with the presence of God. Then the sun slips early behind a mountain and the cold pours fast into your veins. The freeze permeates your bones and opens your eyes to the realization that the land itself is stalking you. Death is around every corner. Alaska appears to be the playground of the gods, but when the cold sets in and the expanse reveals itself as loneliness, the williwaws blow down from the mountains like spirits warning you that you are not supposed to be here. They whisper to you that the only difference between you and the granite stones you stand on is the fire you're hovelled over and the hat that directs the freezing rain away from your head. Without them, you'd be dead. In truth, Alaska is a land God left long ago, and in the groaning of the glaciers one can almost hear the land cry out, "My God, my God, why hast thou forsaken me?" Then the cold overtakes you and the mountains overtower you until you're frightened by the knowledge that you are the last dying ember in a valley of cold stone. On that day, I started to think like Joe. Joe believed God could only do so much, but if your heart was in the right place, he would be ready to receive you when the wilderness finally got the upper hand.

They released me from the hospital two days later. I did not know it at the time, but the hernias, or the surgeries to correct them, left me infertile. My one chance at fatherhood died with the storm. My intestines no longer bulged from my groin, but I was still in a great deal of pain when Joe and I returned to the site of the *Nereid* to scrounge whatever personal items we could find. I was struck by how quickly nature started to erase the mess. The *Nereid* was still there, but so much of the flotsam had disappeared. I looked for the cranberry float, but it had drifted away, perhaps to be found by some other stranger on a distant beach many years in the future. I searched for *Never Cry Wolf* and the pictures Shenan and I had drawn in it, but it was nowhere to be found.

Instead, I found a better memento of Shenan. Inside the hull of the *Nereid*, I discovered her guitar in its hard case, floating in the tide. I grabbed it and found the guitar safe and dry inside. We hauled as much of the junk that we could find—pots and pans, fishing equipment, the stove, and most of the non-biodegradable things that we could lay our hands on. Most of it was thrown away simply to limit the pollution, but I kept the guitar and it became a significant part of my life. I learned to play, then started to write songs—mostly about Alaska and the need to preserve wild places. Because of Shenan, music has infused my life. Often, when playing her guitar, I think of her and I know that she is speaking through the music. In the brief time that I knew her, she manifested in many guises—the Cherokee Mermaid, Salmon Woman, Angeline, the Daughter of the Stars. I used to think that she disappeared in a flash, but the longer I live, the more I believe that the Ghost of the *Mikilak* still haunts Alaska.

# Chapter 20

# Angeline

Late in the afternoon, I finished writing about Shenan and Bristol Bay. Finn and his wife invited me to dinner. Finn's wife, Annie, had been baking all day. The aroma of blueberries filled their log home.

"You've been scarce this week," Annie said when we sat down to dinner.

"Your husband put me to work."

"So, I heard. Was it productive?" She handed me a steaming plate of meat loaf and a fork.

"Very."

"Oh, good. I can't wait to read it."

"This is excellent meat loaf."

"Thank you. And there's blueberry pie for dessert."

"Any word on the Trooper?" Finn asked.

"He's not going to make it till Sunday."

"So, you'll wait then?"

"No. I'll make an attempt tomorrow."

"I see."

"Maybe Finn should go with you."

"No, I don't think so. Finn and I have discussed this. It's my job."

There was a minute of silence before Finn asked, "But you plan to be at the rally, yes?"

"I do."

"What will you speak about?" Annie asked.

"I'm going to talk about the monster."

"The bear?"

"No, I pray that he has not yet become a monster."

"Something you saw in Montana," Finn guessed.

"Yes. The Berkeley Pit, an abandoned open pit copper mine."

"Is it bad?"

"When they turned the pumps off in the 1980's, the groundwater filled it up. It's now a lake that's a thousand feet deep. An acid lake."

"Oh, my."

"I spent a whole day with the men whose only job is to scare the birds away."

Annie's head cocked to the side.

"I'm not making this up. The legal entities that are left after the mining company went out of business assign miners to keep the geese and other birds from landing in the water."

"What happens if they land?"

"They die."

"From what?"

"Drinking the acidic water. They have sirens and hawks and drones and all kinds of things to scare birds because the E.P.A. fines them for every dead goose."

Finn put his fork down. "Is there a dam?"

"No, just the open hole. It's been filling up for years and it's getting close to the water table. There's a depth level that they've determined is the highest the water can reach before it gets into the streams. They call it the Protective Level. Once the water gets that high, they say it will enter the water system."

"How far away is it?"

"About forty feet."

"Out of how many?"

"A thousand."

"Oh, my."

"There's a website called Pitwatch where people can see how high the water is at any given time. They just forced the companies to build a water treatment plant to start siphoning out the water before it reaches the critical level."

"And what if it does?"

"It gets into the streams. The first one is called Silver Bow Creek. And then, of course, into the water that the city of Butte uses."

"That is a monster."

"It's a terrible situation—one that I had to see with my own eyes. I understand that we need mines. The Kennecott Mine turned out okay. But I don't know about the Pebble Mine. Mines must be located in smart places. And this location seems like the worst location possible. Think about it. Where is our Silver Bow Creek? Of the hundreds of streams and lakes around here, which one is the first to get polluted by an abandoned Pebble Mine? This place is like a sponge compared to Butte, Montana."

"You think that will ever happen?" Annie asked.

"I don't know. I never thought ships would be sailing through the Northwest Passage."

"So, you're officially opposed to the mine?" Finn asked.

"Officially, and in all forms. Besides, I thought about something else today."

"The McNeil River?"

"No, I remembered the first time my wife flew over this area, just after we married. There must be places on this earth where people can fly and see a thousand caribou and nothing but wilderness. No road, no equipment, no pipelines. Just wilderness. We can't close off every area to mining. We can't even afford to do that everywhere in Alaska. But there are remote places left where we still can. And if we're going to draw a line in the sand, it might as well be at the greatest salmon fishery in the world."

After a long night of talking and a dessert of blueberry pie, I said good night to the Nickolais and returned to the small cabin behind their house. The tartness of the berries still lingers on my tongue. I don't know if I've ever eaten pie that tasted so good. Now that I have cleared my mind of the Berkeley Pit, tomorrow's mission to track down the bear is weighing down on me. I must take care of that problem before I can tell people what I saw in Montana.

As I walked through the darkness to the cabin, I wondered if I was being reckless. I don't think so. I know that I don't have a death wish. I want to live because there is still so much to learn. Much of the Alaskan wilderness remains a mystery. This lake alone holds many secrets. Lake Iliamna is one of only a few freshwater lakes in the world that is a habitat for seals. When you think about that, it's absurd—seals in a lake. We are not even quite certain what species they are. Do some of them slide up and down the fifty-mile Kvichak River down to Bristol Bay? Or, do they live permanently in the lake? Local knowledge suggests they overwinter in an unknown cave that has underground access to the water, a way for them to slide in and out of the lake when it is covered by ice. I would love to discover this winter rookery, if it exists.

Then, of course, the lake is most famous for being the home of a supposed monster that the locals call Illie. I picture the creature out there in the water now. It is a dark night, but I have a fine view of the lake. I can see the inky, mercurial waters of Pedro Bay where in 1977 a pilot reported seeing a 14-foot fish that flicked its massive tail before diving into the depths. That is only one of scores of sightings I could recount. Is that fish, or one of its offspring, out there skimming the dark waters right now unbeknownst to the humans huddled together in this tiny village? What of the sightings that report a thirty-foot animal? What of the native legends—tales of a giant beast called Gonakadet with the body of an orca and head and tail of a wolf?

I am fairly convinced there is some truth to these legends. Likely, some species of sturgeon or sleeper shark inhabits these waters. It sounds strange, but freshwater seals are just as unlikely. The white sturgeon of North America can reach twenty feet in length and more than 1,500 pounds. The tough scales on a sturgeon's back could account for the "bite marks" reported on the props of boats that have supposedly run into Illie. On the other hand, Pacific Sleeper Sharks, the enormous black beasts that prowl the ocean depths, have been found in brackish water around Bristol Bay. Though they are generally thought to be slow animals, fresh salmon have been found in their stomachs indicating they can somehow prey upon swift species. In fact, nearly every kind of arctic mammal has been found in the bellies of sleeper sharks—from baby polar bears to seals. If seals live in this lake, perhaps sharks do, too. In a lake that is a thousand feet deep with a thousand square miles of water, only God knows what creatures lurk beneath its surface.

I do not know if such a creature exists, but I do know that another dangerous creature is prowling the land not far from here. He is wounded and hungry, and perhaps scared. He has learned that humans can be food. He is desperate and therefore unpredictable, and I must find him, and the weight of the task presses down upon me now. I know that the second trooper won't be here tomorrow. I know that I should wait for him, but if the bear hurts one more person, a witch hunt would ensue. The events would turn into stories, and the stories would grow into legends, and legends change how societies think and act. The black-faced bear would become another Beast of the Gevaudan—the supposed monster that attacked scores of people in a remote region of France in the 1760's. After years of living in terror and after a hundred people had been killed, King Louis XV sent his gunbearer to deal with the situation. It was not until the gunbearer killed several large wolves in the region that the killings stopped. By then, stories of a mythic creature had developed, and we live with those stories still. There was no reason to invent a creature with monstrous features when real monsters had developed. Most conservationists would not use the word monster to describe an animal, but I believe in them. The vast majority of large predators are benign toward humans, but when they lose their fear of us, and especially when they learn that we are slow, weak, and edible, their natural tastes and inclinations are perverted. It is then that they become monsters. They are rare, but they are very real.

I have killed more than a few bears in my life, but my sight and hearing aren't what they used to be. I am slower and weaker than I once was, and my sense of balance has deteriorated quickly over the past year. I am as likely to fall and break my neck as I am to be attacked by the black-faced bear. My mind conjures many ways to die out there, and the worst thought is that I know that one of them will actually happen in the near future. If not tomorrow, then within a few years, maybe a decade. What will happen to me when I'm gone? Will Shenan be there? Did she find some happy hunting ground in the sky? Some might say that her beliefs differed radically from my own. That's what I thought when I knew her. I spoke of God and his will. She spoke of the universe and its plan. I talked to her of heaven. She spoke of reincarnation. But over the years, I've come to think that we mostly believed in the same things. We both looked forward to life after this. Did we differ in this as much as I once supposed?

Moments ago, I cleaned the barrel of my old Winchester .45-70. I thought the ritual might prepare me for sleep. It didn't. Acid lakes and monsters lurk in the corners of my mind. I picked up my Bible and read by the light of the oil lamp. Usually, I find comfort in this, but some feeling gnawed at me. Then, it struck me. It's not anxiety that's bothering me now. It is loneliness. All this writing about Shenan opened the hole she left when she died. I've often dreamed of what our lives would have been like together. In these dreams, I am still a biologist. She is sometimes a teacher, sometimes a camp counselor. I picture her mentoring hundreds of children at wilderness camps. Sometimes we have our own children. But always she is a warrior for conservation fighting against the sprawling electric grid and the coal mines. I have pictured her protesting with signs along the highway and speaking at town halls. I picture her gardening and relaxing in hot springs with me. Always, we live in a cabin together. Always, we are happy.

Over the years, I stopped playing these games, for they left me with that feeling—this feeling—this hollowness inside, this thought that I want to see her again. And now, almost in response to my thoughts, I hear a comforting sound. It does not pierce the night. It does not fill the sky. It comes like a long finger from a dark ridge somewhere in the forest. It winds its way past my airplane, through the open window of the cabin, and touches me gently on the ear. It is the sad, almost human-like howl of a wolf, pitching high then low, moaning up into the cold, thin air of the night. It is Angeline. Despite my hopes that she would move on, she lingers near me, calling to me, telling me that I will not be alone on the long, treacherous trail ahead. I smile toward the window and the star-bright sky beyond. I'm coming, Angeline, I tell her. I'm coming. But first I must get some sleep, because in the morning we hunt for bear.

# ACKNOWLEDGMENTS

The author would like to acknowledge:

My fishing boat skippers, Steve Lewis of the Aventura, and Joe Meier and his brother, Bob, of the Apollo. Thanks for taking me onboard and showing me the ropes.

Bob Durr, for his book Down in Bristol Bay (1999). While I am intimately familiar with Bristol Bay gillnetting, I leaned on his book for insights into fishing in the late 1960s. It is a good book and worth the read.

My editor and distributor, Flip Todd, for taking on the project and helping me to create the very best product possible.

Author and friend, Vicki Berger Erwin, who believed in my writing early, even when it wasn't my best stuff. I will forever be thankful for her edits and sage counsel.

My friend, Christopher Wooldridge, whose knowledge about writing and story-crafting was indispensable in editing this book, and especially for believing that it was a story worth telling.

My brother, Caleb Keil, who has been my closest collaborator for more than a decade. Thank you for reading and editing all the different versions of the book. You never once made me lose faith in it.

My wife, Stacie, who has been my stalwart and loving companion through the highs and the lows, and for always encouraging me.